the
SMUDGER

ANGELINE TREVENA

Bogus Caller Press

ISBN: 978-0-9934864-4-9

Cover art by Oliviaprodesign

Published by Bogus Caller Press
www.boguscallerpress.co.uk

Publisher's note:
The Smudger is a work of fiction. All names,
characters, and places are the product of the author's
imagination, used in fictitious manner. Any
resemblances to actual persons, places, locales,
events, etc. are purely coincidental.

ALSO BY ANGELINE TREVENA

Cutting the Bloodline

The Notary of Gotliss Street

The Paper Duchess Series:

The Bottle Stopper

The Matching

The Visionary

The Mothers

The Memory Trader Series:

The Stray

The Smudger

The Sister

Poisonmarch Series:

After: A Post Apocalyptic Story Collection

While We Were Waiting

Lobaya
(Arukumbi)

• Aojima

(Katu)
(Kalu) • (Gele)
(Juwezi)
(Jukapa) (Arumina)
(Kolpanga)
(Kiba)

• Nagamoto

Kanaoka
(Kumini)

• Naradai

• Miyakata

• Akimori

Honporo
(Mitmanimba)

Iwoyo (Kamena)

• Kumonayo

Okaporo
(Juire)

• Kagosaka

Nagaporo
(Wasi)

PART ONE

1

KIOTO

I peaked my hand across my forehead and squinted at the wallowing city ahead. I didn't want to be here. I avoided the cities when I could. I liked the cool, quiet woods, the desolate moors, the vast, empty expanses of land where I could almost believe that I was entirely alone in the world. But, sometimes, venturing into these stinking hell-holes was an unavoidable chore.

It wasn't even the city itself that bothered me. In a city I could disappear, I could move around almost completely unseen. People didn't want to see my kind, and so, they didn't. They had become so adept at ignoring us that we existed only in blind spots.

What bothered me was the colonies. Half-built shanty towns that clung to the edges of the cities like unwelcome pustules. So desperate to belong, to be accepted, but they would never be viewed as anything other than blemishes. If it could, the city would have picked them off like leeches and tossed them back to the swamps and marshlands it believed they came from.

It was in one of these colonies that I had been born, grown up, been educated. Learnt how to be a memory trader; taking people's unwanted memories to sell onto someone who might make use of them. I knew all the colony ways, and I didn't want to be a part them. My colony had been torn apart, and I'd never found anywhere else that felt even remotely like a home.

But the two sausages wrapped in a piece of half-stale bread I'd had for breakfast was the last of my food, and now, already late afternoon, hunger had won out.

I hitched my bag further onto my back, bowed my head and trudged on towards civilisation.

I'd barely stepped into the colony before a child slipped a hand into mine. She looked up at me, grinning out from under a mop of curls.

"What's your name?" she asked.

"Kioto." I replied.

The girl twisted her head around and called out to someone I couldn't see. "She is! I told you so!"

She turned her eager eyes back to me. "Are you a trader?"

I pushed back my hair to show her the traditional scars that marked my face. That and my name were the only things my parents had ever given me, and both of them marked me as what I was.

Another two children joined us; a girl and a boy.

"Did you see them?" the boy asked.

The first girl nodded enthusiastically, her hair bouncing back and forth. "She showed me." Her chest swelled. I sneered. It was hardly something to be proud of.

"What colony are you from?"

I thought for a moment. Where was I from? Okaporo was long gone, and if these children had heard of it, it wouldn't have been pleasant stories. And I would never claim to be from Kagosaka. They never claimed me as one of their own, so I wasn't going to extend that courtesy.

"I don't belong to a colony," I replied.

I watched the look of confusion crease her face. "What do you mean?"

"I mean I don't belong to a colony. I'm a wandering trader."

"But all traders belong to a colony," said the boy.

"Why won't you tell us?" the second girl said. "Is it a secret?"

"Maybe she's a spy," the boy offered.

"I'm not a spy. I just don't belong to a colony. You can do that, you know."

The questions came thick and fast then, and I soon found myself surrounded by a small crowd of children ranging from toddlers to teenagers.

"Where do you live?"

"How do you find jobs?"

"What do you eat?"

"Were you banished?"

"Are you a rogue?"

"Do the High still watch over you?"

"Do you still perform the Grace?"

"Yes, I perform the Grace," I said, a little too sharply. The children drew back as one. "The High still watch over me, and they always will. No matter where I sleep at night."

"And they always know where you are?"

"Of course they do." A teenage girl answered that question for me, and the whole group quietened. "They know everything. They see everything. They see right into our souls. There's no hiding from them." She slapped the enquirer across the back of the head. "You need to pay more attention in your classes."

The boy in question rubbed his cranium. "I do, I know."

"Then you'll also know that the High know she's abandoned her colony, abandoned the true path, and that her soul will pay for that for all eternity." She focussed her sharp eyes on me. "Isn't that right?"

I shrugged. "If that's what you believe."

"That is the truth. Your colony would never abandon you."

I cocked my head. Little did she know. "Then you stick to that. You have your path, and I have mine. Let's be happy with that."

She took hold of my wrist then, and we all stopped walking. "There is only one path," she said.

"I suggest you let go of me," I said, trying to

sound as menacing as I could. The truth was, this girl terrified me. Her unfaltering belief, her blinkered self-righteousness, her influence over the others. I suspected the colony's brood mother was her grandmother, or great grandmother. She scared me because I saw, in her, the reflection of who I was supposed to be. Who I would have been made into if anyone had cared enough to do it.

"I hope you're making our visitor feel welcome." At the sound of that voice, the children scattered. Even the girl released her grip on my arm and turned, hands folded in front of her, head bowed.

The brood mother pushed the girl aside and slipped her hand into the crook of my elbow, drawing me to one side.

"I think we'd better talk in private," she said. She steered me towards one of the buildings. She moved a beaded curtain to one side, the wooden clacking of it like static in my brain, and gestured for me to go inside.

If there had been a catalogue of traditional furnishings for a brood mother's home, this would have been one of the pages in it.

Against one wall stood her altar, kitted out with everything an altar should have. Arced around the back was a line of twelve stones; representing each member of the High. Hung behind them was the embroidered image of the setting sun. Or the rising sun perhaps. To be honest, I'd never been certain as to which it was supposed to represent. I guess it all depended on your point of view.

Everything else was present and correct, lined up perfectly. The bowl of water placed in the north, the sprig of heather in the west, the rabbit pelt in the south, and in the east, the pebble. These things represented the four sanctities: life, roots, family, and influence.

The floor was covered in several overlapping rugs; thick and intricately patterned. There were a number of large cushions scattered around, each sporting a fringe of coloured tassels. I could see how that girl had become so self-righteous. The colony could be held up as a shining example of how to do things properly.

The brood mother was pouring me a tea before I could politely refuse. I hated the stuff, always had, it tasted like it had been dredged from the bottom of a stagnant pool. But it was tradition, and so, when she offered me the small bowl, I took it with a smile and a nod.

She raised her own bowl to me. "Ever watchful," she said.

"Ever watchful," I repeated, although that phrase had come to mean something completely different to me over the years.

I closed my eyes and took a sip of the steaming liquid, thankful that the bowls were only small. The tea wasn't drunk to quench thirst, it was drunk simply because things had always been done that way. After drinking the dreadful stuff, people tended to open a bottle of wine, or hand out the beers. Maybe everyone found it as distasteful as I did. The difference was, I didn't see the point in doing something unpleasant simply because of tradition.

The brood mother gestured for me to sit on one of the cushions, and I sank to the floor. I gulped the rest of my tea down and handed her the empty bowl. She looked at it for a moment before taking it.

"Passing through?" she asked.

"Looking for a job. My purse is a little light. Well, empty, in fact."

"Then we better do what we can to see you on your way quickly then."

She wasn't offering her help out of kindness, or solidarity for her people. She was simply keen to get rid of me.

"I'm sorry about talking to the kids," I said. "I got somewhat ambushed."

"You shouldn't fill their heads with ridiculous ideas."

"I was simply answering their questions."

"With radical, rebellious notions."

I couldn't help but smile. "Just because my view is different, it doesn't make it rebellious."

"We are a close-knit colony. We rely on one another. That may be something you don't understand, but it is something we promote. Something we teach to those youngsters. You may have just undone years of teachings."

I sighed. "I hardly think—"

"Children are sponges. You're a novelty, and that's exciting to them. Attractive even. You offer them an alternative way to view the world and, at best, they get confused. At worse, they get dangerous ideas about how things could be."

"They should be thinking about the way things could be. That's how change happens. That's how we move forward. How we evolve."

The brood mother pressed her lips together. "Don't think I haven't heard about you. I know exactly who you are, Kioto. While my heart aches for your past, I cannot condone your present. And your presence is not welcome here."

I nodded. This was hardly a new experience. I'd been dragged into the houses of so many brood mothers, been asked to leave from so many colonies. I was impressed by how many ways they knew to politely say 'you're not welcome here'.

"Believe me, I have no intention of staying. Like I said, I'm looking for a job, and then I'll be on my way."

"I'll get someone to take you into the city, show you where the exchange is."

"And make sure I don't come back, eh?"

She huffed.

I pushed myself to my feet and swung my bag back over my shoulder. "Fine. Thanks for your help."

"And next time, you'll know where it is. So you won't need to come here and ask, will you?"

I rolled my eyes. She was certainly keen to get her message across. "Of course not. Thanks for your hospitality."

Outside, a single gesture from the brood mother brought a woman hurrying over. Her hair was tightly plaited back from her face to proudly show off her scars.

"Take Kioto to the exchange for me."

They nodded a silent understanding to one another.

"Thanks again," I said. As I walked away I couldn't help calling "see you again soon" over my shoulder.

We walked in silence for some time before curiosity finally overcame.

"Kioto?" the woman asked. "As in Kioto from...?" She drifted off, it was a sentence people rarely wanted to finish.

I helped her out. "From Okaporo, yes, that's me. It appears my reputation precedes me once again."

She placed a hand over her heart. "My heart aches for you."

I nodded politely. I was fed up of hearing it. And it wasn't as if it was ever truly meant. That's why I never introduced myself, why I never told anyone where I was from. First I got the look of sympathy, then that flash of fear when they realised they had to say something that sounded sincere. Luckily, there was always a default response to use. Memory traders were good at that; creating scripts so that no one ever had to actually say something from the heart.

"Is it true? That you don't belong to a colony?"

"It is."

"How does that work?"

"I go where I want. I sleep where I can. I eat when I can. And I work when I need to. It's far less complicated."

"I admire you."

I looked at her. "You admire me?"

She nodded. "You're so brave. And you're free. Totally free."

I laughed. "I guess your brood mother sent the wrong person with me. Remember your pebble? Don't let me put a nick in that nice smooth surface."

"I'm afraid I don't have much of a smooth surface left. I probably never had one. I ran with the rogues for a while."

I stopped and stared at her. "Wait. What?"

"It's true. I'm still not entirely certain which side I want to be on."

"Look, I hate colony life, but there's a big difference between—"

"It's so romantic," she cut in. "Being rebellious. Being free."

"Romantic?" My voice squeaked out of my tight throat. Memories fizzled in my brain, rising back to the surface, piercing through every attempt I made to bury them. "Romantic?" I repeated.

"Well, I know that they—" She clamped her hand over her mouth. "I'm so sorry," she spluttered through her fingers. "I can't believe I just…"

I placed my hand on her chest. "You can save your scripted gestures and your rehearsed sentiments. If you think having everyone you ever loved or trusted massacred is romantic then…then…" There weren't any words for this. "I'll find the exchange myself."

2

SENETSU

The chair creaked underneath me as I leant back and closed my eyes against the glare of the afternoon sun. It was just an old garden chair scavenged from somewhere. The seat sported a few frayed holes, and the frame was rusted at every joint, but in a place where everyone seemed to prefer sitting on the ground, it was a rare luxury.

As was this. A sunny afternoon with nothing to do. There always seemed to be some kind of chore or favour to be done, and if anyone spotted me in a moment of idleness, they always quickly found me something to occupy my time.

I opened my eyes a crack, filtering the sunlight through my lashes, and watched my girls play. I'd managed to trade an extraction job for a doll's house and a handful of dolls. There wasn't much furniture for it, and we'd had to make clothes for half of the dolls to protect their modesty, but it was the best toy they'd ever had, and they'd played with it endlessly. It was the envy of every other child in the colony, and their absolute pride.

I closed my eyes again. I deserved a moment of idleness before they started arguing again. Separately, they were angels. But whenever they were together, arguments quickly flared.

"Mama."

I opened one eye. Kioto was tugging at my skirt.

"Yes, Kioto?"

"When are lessons starting today?"

"There are no lessons today. Remember?"

"Why?"

I sat up. The scars over her eye were still red, but they'd fade in time. I'd hated doing it, but it was my duty, and the colonies placed a heavy importance on duties.

"Because Miya and the other rooks are having a meeting with Narata. I told you this morning."

"What are they having a meeting about?"

"I don't know. But when it's important that we do know, we'll be told."

"Is it secret?"

I shrugged. "I guess so."

"But aren't secrets bad?"

"Some secrets are bad. But some secrets have to be kept to protect people. That's Narata's job as brood mother. She has to protect us. And if that means keeping secrets, then that's what she has to do. And we trust her, right?"

Kioto nodded. "Right."

"So you can go back to playing now."

I leant back and closed my eyes, but I could almost hear Kioto thinking things over, and I braced myself for another question.

"When will we find out?"

"That's Narata's decision, not mine."

"When she tells us, will she tell us that it was what they talked about at this meeting? Otherwise, we might think it's just new information, not secret information, and we might not realise that it's this secret information that we're being told. And we'll still be waiting for that, because we won't realise we've already been told it."

I sat back up. "What?"

Kioto cocked her head and looked up at me with surprise. She sighed a sigh with her entire body in a way that only children approaching their teenage years can.

"Forget it," she said. "You don't understand." She turned and skipped back to where her sister was still playing.

I shook my head.

My phone pinged and I pulled it out of my pocket.

'LIBERATION! Hide the girls.'

"Kioto! Omori!" I cried. "Liberation!"

They didn't need telling twice. This was the one

and only instruction that they both obeyed without question, without turning it into a debate or a negotiation. It was a regularly practised drill, although Kioto had only done it for real once before, and this was Omori's first time. Both girls ran into the house without fuss. Kioto pushed aside the sofa, using her entire body, and lifted the trapdoor beneath. She stepped down into the darkness beneath it and lifted Omori in after her. They both crouched down, their faces turned upwards as I closed the lid over them.

"Keep still," I whispered to them. "Keep quiet." I pushed the sofa back into place.

Although my heart was threatening to break out of my chest, I managed to walk quietly outside. I glanced around, and froze as I spotted the doll's house sat, like a guilty plea, in the open. I looked towards the gates and saw the cars already pulling in, armed officers climbing out before the vehicles even came to a complete stop. I didn't have time to hide it. I grabbed the chair and tossed it towards the house. I winced as it collided, sheering the roof right off and splitting the back wall into pieces.

"What's that?"

I stared at my reflection in the buttons on the officer's jacket and put on my best expression of wilfulness.

"Why've you come in your posh stuff?" I asked.

"What's that?" he repeated.

"I mean, you guys only wear this fancy shiny-buttoned stuff for ceremonies and marches. It's not your everyday uniform, is it? Why would you get all dressed up to come out to a colony?"

"Do you want to be arrested?"

"For what?"

"Obstruction." He took hold of my chin in his gloved hand and turned my face towards the buckled chair and the broken doll's house. "What's that?"

"Looks like a pile of rubbish to me. Did you want to have a rummage? It's amazing what people throw out."

He marched over to it without releasing his grip on my face. I shuffled and scuffed along, trying not to trip over his boots. He turned me towards it again.

"It looks like children's toys," he said.

"Broken children's toys," I corrected.

"It's a criminal offence to hide colony children from the authorities. The Liberation Scheme is for their benefit. They'll be raised properly, re-educated, given proper chances in life. Wouldn't you want the best for your children?"

"I would if I had any left. You already took mine. If you checked your little screen, you'd already know that."

He finally let go of me, wiping his hand on his trousers. With a grunt, he kicked at the doll's house, splitting the middle floor in half.

"Clear this up," he said. "It's a health and safety hazard."

3

KIOTO

Trader exchanges weren't difficult to find. You simply followed the smell to the worst part of the city, and then looked for the worst of the worst part. When you thought it couldn't get any dirtier, more disgusting, or depraved, that was where you'd find the exchange.

The grubby sign swung back and forth above the door sporting a crude scrawling of an eye crossed with three lines. The traditional trader emblems had long ago been replaced with this debased image, making the exchanges easier to find and identify. Because that's all citizens saw us as: three scars over one eye. Why pretend we were anything more?

I pushed the door open and stepped inside. The small, cramped space doubled as some kind of café, with a couple of small tables pushed against one wall, surrounded by mismatched chairs. Exchanges couldn't get by without diversifying anymore. Most citizens preferred to hire the merchants; those that had broken away from the colonies, opting for life within the cities instead of clinging to the edge of them. The few jobs left for colony traders were poorly paid, unwanted, or just illegal.

A couple of screens flickered on the wall behind the desk, updating with available jobs as they were submitted via the trader network. Kioto joined the few traders already standing there, and cast her eyes over the vacancies.

Each job that appeared disappeared just as quickly. This wasn't the only exchange in the city, and the merchants had instant access to the network via their screens. They didn't have to come to places like this to find work. They just sat on their plush sofas in their designer homes and logged straight in.

The merchants also benefited from access to the alpha network. But to get access to that, you needed an address inside the city limits. The better jobs were only posted there.

So here I was, at the exchange, with everyone else at the bottom of the food chain.

"861A!" I shouted loudly, even making myself

jump. The woman behind the desk swiped the job from the screen, dragging the details onto a cyber card for me. She tossed it onto the counter, and I touched my phone to the pay pad. It double-bleeped as I did so, indicating that my account was near its limit.

The woman looked at me with sympathy. "Better hurry, looks like you really need this one, and you don't want it getting poached."

I glanced at the other traders next to me.

"It's not them you need to worry about," the woman behind the counter clarified. "It's the merchants."

"They have their own jobs, they're not interested in these."

"No, they wouldn't be normally. But recently, they seem to be logging in and stealing them just out of spite."

I grabbed the cyber card from the counter and held it up to the light. The first route instruction was already flashing. All I had to do was follow.

4

KIOTO

The address was modest, but a larger house than I would have expected. People with this kind of property tended to post their jobs on the alpha network to avoid any undesirables knocking at their door.

As I walked up the short drive, however, I noticed that the grass was overgrown, and brambles tangled around the bottoms of the trees. Weeds were springing up from the gravel beneath my feet.

The house also looked like it needed some attention. Peeling paint, missing roof tiles, dull, dirty windows. The property was clearly getting too much to handle. It was likely an unwanted inheritance kept in the family out of duty rather than desire.

I turned the last corner of the drive, and the full house came into view. In the centre of the drive, an old fountain sputtered water that splashed over a chipped and stained basin. Behind that stood a merchant's wagon.

As I approached the front door, it swung open, and the merchant stepped out. He beamed at me, lifting his hand to touch his hat in a mock show of courtesy. His smug smile confirmed my fears.

"What's going on?" I asked.

"It seems," said the merchant, "that your services are no longer required."

I looked past him to the client who had frozen mid-handshake.

"What's going on?" I repeated.

The man shrugged, his face reddening. "He turned up first...ah...I...I didn't know if you were coming."

"I've just spent half my journey here talking to you. Figuring out details. You knew full well that I was on my way."

"You should've been quicker, dear," the merchant put in. "Perhaps if you had a car, or even used public transport. I hear it's really quite luxurious these days. Not that I'd know myself, of course."

"Shut it," I spat. I turned back to the client. "This isn't how things are done."

"This is business," the merchant said.

"Why did you even want this job in the first place?" I snapped at him.

He shrugged, his fat neck disappearing into the wide collar of his coat for a moment. "Something to pass the time. Now, if you'll excuse me, I have a rather niggly memory to offload." He looked over at his wagon. "Now...who to choose, who to choose."

I stepped towards the client and lowered my voice. "This isn't how things are done. We had a deal. I really needed this job."

The colour of the man's face deepened even further. He stared at the floor, shuffled his feet. "I'm sorry. I don't know what else to say."

"You have no honour."

"Perhaps you should leave," the merchant said. "You've no business here. Quite literally."

My hands clenched involuntarily, and it took all of my concentration to stop myself from burying my fists into his fat, smug face.

"I'm not speaking to you."

"I'm sorry," the client said again. "Please leave, otherwise I..." he trailed off.

"What? You'll have me arrested? What about you? For breach of contract."

"We only had a verbal one. Just a chat on the phone. Nothing was definite."

"Look, chick," the merchant said, "you missed out. It happens. But now you're just embarrassing yourself. Go back to your colony and put it down to experience."

I looked back at the client. "C'mon, I really needed this."

"I'm sorry." He shuffled backwards and closed

the door.

"Can I give you a lift somewhere?" the merchant asked.

"No thank you."

He sighed with breath that stank of fried chicken. "Look, swallow your pride and take an offer of help. This—" he gestured towards the house "—this was just business. You know that. But this is a genuine offer. Maybe I could buy you something to eat too."

"I don't need your charity."

"Then let me do you a favour. I know of a job that might be well suited to your talents. Let me get you the details."

Lifting his hands, he pulled out a box shape in the air between his fingers and thumbs. The implants under his skin created a screen in the air.

"I don't have a screen," I said. I pulled my phone from my pocket and held it out to him.

He nodded. "Of course. I forget you people still live like that. Let me get you the man's card."

He strode over towards his wagon and, reluctantly, I followed. I didn't even want a job from him, but my stomach was aching with hunger, and it had been a long walk from the exchange. Cities in Lobaya were monstrously large, and it had taken me almost two hours to get here on foot.

I looked up at his wagon. The back was mostly boxed in, but an open slit ran around the side of it. You might think he was transporting animals if it weren't for the voices and the hands reaching out towards me. I shuddered. I couldn't understand how anyone could look at one human and think 'human', and then look at another and think 'slave' or 'object'. But that was how the world was.

He opened the door on the cab and dragged his briefcase to the edge of the seat. He flicked it open and dug through the contents. He held a cyber card out to me. After a moment's hesitation, I took it from him. It wouldn't harm to take the card, even though I had no intention of following up on it.

"Go see this guy," the merchant said. "Tell him Cota sent you. You won't even get in otherwise. He's...er...off network."

I stepped backwards, my head shaking wildly. "No, I don't do that stuff. I'm not a ripper. Only legitimate jobs."

"Just think it over. When was the last time you ate? Or showered? Or slept in a proper bed?"

"I'm not a ripper."

He shrugged and pushed the briefcase away. "Your choice." He twitched. "If you'll excuse me, I really need to get rid of this memory."

I looked at the hands stretching out of the wagon. One of his slaves would be loaded with that memory until he could sell it on. That's how merchants worked. They did very little of the work themselves.

It wasn't comfortable to carry someone else's memory. It was like wearing someone else's shoes. At first, it just feels a little odd, the soles are worn down in a different pattern because of the way they walk. But, eventually, you find yourself walking more like them to match the shoes. Their walk starts to become a part of you. And it was like that with memories. Holding on to too many, or keeping them for too long would send you crazy.

I nodded and turned away, walking down past the wagon. As I did, a hand grabbed my shoulder, and pressed its fingers into my neck.

In that moment, a memory flicked into my brain. Just a whisper of it, just a fleeting glimpse. It can happen sometimes, especially when the person touching you is topped out with memories. But what I saw, what I felt and heard, was proof that the last eleven years of my life had been a lie.

I turned back to Cota. "I want to buy your smudger," I said.

5

KIOTO

Cota grinned broadly and folded his hands over his chest. "Do you now?" he said.

"How much?" I asked.

"She's almost topped out."

"I know."

"So she won't come cheap."

I frowned. "But she's barely usable."

"Not as a slave, at least."

"What else would I use her for?"

He winked at me, and I actually stepped back in surprise. I couldn't even imagine what other use she might have. She was stuffed full of bad memories that were making her crazy, giving her the shivers.

"How much?" I pressed.

He nodded his head from side to side for a moment, weighing up the question. "Five hundred."

I laughed, but he kept his face straight. "You're serious?"

"Five hundred."

"But she's useless."

"Five hundred."

"I can't get hold of that kind of money."

Cota shrugged. "Ah well."

I quickly thought things through. "How long can you give me?"

"Two days." He held up two thick fingers. "I'm only visiting, and I'll be moving on."

"How can I get five hundred in two days?"

He pointed towards the cyber card I still held in my hand.

"Can you give me more time?"

"Absolutely not. I'm on a schedule. Two days." He held his fingers up again.

I looked down at the cyber card in my hand. "I'll get your money. But not like this. I'm not a ripper."

Cota shrugged again. "Then good luck to you."

6

SENETSU

I shifted Omori on my hip and waited outside Narata's door. She'd summoned me, which was far from regular.

"Come on, get down, you're heavy." I put Omori on the floor, but she still grabbed at my leg, asking to be lifted up. "You're a big girl now, you can stand by yourself." It came out sharper than I'd intended.

I turned as I heard footsteps behind us.

"You've been summoned as well?" I asked Saji as he approached.

"Daddy!" chorused Omori, running to him with her arms outstretched. He scooped her up, rolled her upside down, and finally sat her up on his shoulders. She looked at me with a grin. I sighed.

"And I thought she'd only summoned me," he said. "I'd assumed it was something to do with the farm."

"Now I'm really worried."

"I'm sure it's nothing." He took hold of my hand and squeezed it. "Probably another glowing report of Kioto's impressive progress."

"I wish I could be as relaxed as you."

He winked at me. That was just like him. No matter what trouble befell him, he always faced it with an annoyingly casual smile and, more annoyingly, he always seemed to breeze through it. I, on the other hand, spent every moment thinking up every possible worse case scenario, usually to discover that things weren't nearly as bad as I thought. A natural worrier. But then, men didn't have too much to worry about. Only women could become traders in the colonies, and they were responsible for training up the girls, they ran the council, the finances, the admin, everything. The men worked the land and fathered children. And that was pretty much it for them. So they could afford their casual smiles. I could not.

The door to Narata's house creaked open, and her face appeared in the gap. She smiled widely, perhaps trying to reassure me, but I saw the worry in her eyes.

"Come in," she said, opening the door wider.

We stepped inside, and even Saji quietened in the atmosphere of solemnity. Omori, however, remained oblivious, and found her way to Narata's cabinet of treasures. It was a small chest of tiny drawers, each filled with exciting things to explore: nuts, pine cones, buttons, seeds. It never failed to keep children amused while the adults had business to get done.

Narata took hold of one of my hands, and one of Saji's, and clasped them together.

"I knew when I chose Saji for you that it would be for keeps," she said. "That he would do anything for you. Protect you. And now you have two beautiful girls."

"What's this about, Narata?" My heart was hammering so hard I was sure everyone must be able to hear it.

Narata squeezed my hand. "Always the worrier."

"Well, I'm sure you didn't summon us both here to reminisce our marriage."

Narata closed her eyes and nodded. "You're right. I have a very grave matter to discuss. An important mission. One that can only be given to the two of you." She opened her eyes and glanced past us to where Omori was playing. "I need you to leave Okaporo. This colony is no longer safe for you."

"What do you mean, 'leave'?"

Narata took a deep breath, and took forever to exhale it. I'd never wanted to hit a woman before now. Never.

"The rogues know that the vessel is here. And they're coming for it."

"When?"

"Now."

"Now?"

"In a matter of minutes, I'd guess."

I looked at Saji, and then at our daughter. She had no idea what was happening. That her whole world was about to be turned upside down.

"How did they find out?" Saji asked.

"I don't know," said Narata.

"How do we know this? Is this information reliable?" I asked.

"I trust in it completely. So I need you both to leave, straight away. Take the vessel to Kumonayo. Tokai, the brood mother there, will be expecting you."

"Kumonayo? That's the other side of the country. It's not even a sister colony."

"It's the only place that's safe for you right now."

I looked at Saji. "We need to get Kioto. Pack our things."

"There's no time," Narata said.

"We can't take anything?"

"There's simply not time. And Kioto is away at her lessons. Miya's taken her up to to Iwoyo. There's just no time."

The hammering of my heart stopped then. It froze in that moment; pumping neither in nor out. The whole world stalled. The sea paused in its eternal cycle, the wind hushed, the clouds ceased their passage across the sky. Even the sun dimmed.

"There's no time? To collect our daughter?"

"I'm sorry, Senetsu, but there's no choice. You must protect the vessel, and that means leaving Kioto behind."

"Leaving her to what? Death?"

"She's safely away, as are all of the students. Okaporo will live on. And she will be a part of its rebuilding. Okaporo will need her."

"She's eight years old," said Saji.

Narata nodded towards Omori. "And she's only four. Yet she carries the burden of the entire future on those little shoulders."

"No," I said. "We carry that burden for her. You can't expect Kioto to—" All of our phones pinged. We didn't need to read the message to know what it said.

"You need to go," said Narata. "You need to go now or it will be too late. It will all be for nothing. The traders will lose the vessel and you... You will lose your beautiful little girl, and Kioto will still be all alone. You have a chance to save them both, even if you can't take them both with you."

"You're asking us to choose between our children," Saji said.

"No," I replied. "We're not even getting a choice."

"None of us have a choice anymore," Narata said.

My body went cold. "What about the rest of you?"

Narata shook her head slowly. "There's just no time. The vessel is the only important one." She looked over at Omori. "We must protect her at all cost. All cost."

"Come with us."

Narata shook her head again. "I'll only slow you down."

I grabbed her and pulled her tight up against me.

Narata had been present my whole life. A second mother, grandmother. I couldn't imagine existing without her. It was like saying goodbye to my own shadow.

"Ever watchful," I whispered in her ear.

And then I let her go. I scooped up my daughter, and we left, amid the swelling sound of engines.

We ran south, heading for the mountains. I'd never seen them, but I could already feel their presence, looming, invisible, ahead of us. I could feel the cold pressing towards us, their hard edges, their featureless faces. And behind us, the cool ocean. The only home I'd ever had. The only family I'd ever known. Everyone who loved me. Everyone I loved. My daughter. Part of me would always be in Okaporo. I wondered if I'd ever be complete again.

Next to me, Saji breathed hard, and Omori whimpered as she jolted up and down in his arms. We hadn't even brought a coat for her.

When our throats burned, and our legs shook from the exertion, we stopped. We turned back to Okaporo, and let the wind blow smoke into our faces. Our home was in flames. Our people were burning. We heard the crackle of gunfire, an explosion.

And still my heart did not beat. I vowed that it never would again.

7

KIOTO

When I returned to the exchange, I was relieved to find it empty. The woman behind the desk looked up and smiled grimly.

"No luck?"

I shook my head. "They decided to go with a different provider."

"Bloody basers. I'm sorry love, they're all at it these days."

I pulled my phone from my pocket and laid it on the counter. "Look, I don't have enough money to pay for another job."

"Don't worry, I'll refund the last one."

"Really? That would be great, thank you so much." She was under no obligation to do that, but in tough times, you looked after your community. And however much I tried to distance myself from it, this was my community.

"Choose another one, free of charge." She gestured towards the screens behind her. "Not that there's much choice on offer, I'm afraid."

"There never is for people like us," I said. "I'll take 543G."

She loaded the information onto a cyber card and handed it to me.

"Thanks," I said. "I'll see you soon."

"Sticking round for a few days, are you?"

I rolled my eyes. "A couple, I guess."

"Well, I hope you have better luck with this one."

"Thanks."

The address wasn't far; a third floor property in an undesirable part of the city. I stood on the pavement outside and looked up at the block. Every instinct told me to walk away, that something wasn't right. But, unless I was willing to sell my soul and take an illegal job, I didn't have much choice.

I stepped up to the door and ran my cyber card across the reader. It automatically announced my arrival. Somewhere up above me, a robotic woman's voice would chirp, 'You have a caller from the exchange. Would you like to grant access?' The door beside me buzzed, and I pushed it open. I checked the cyber card. Number 34.

The building's hallway was functional and characterless. A small curved desk stood at one side, but there was no sign of security, if there ever had been any. It didn't seem like the sort of place that would hire someone to watch who came in and out. It didn't look like the sort of place that even cared.

I pressed the button for the lift, and waited. Nothing. No lights, no whirr of machinery. No indication that it was operational. I looked around for the stairs. I'd have to do this the old-fashioned way. Luckily, my entire life had prepared me for having to do things the hard way.

The stairway and upstairs landings were decorated with the same formality as the hallway. Completely inoffensive, nothing to cause controversy.

I knocked on the door.

"Are you the trader?" A voice called from the other side of it.

"Yes," I called back hesitantly.

I listened as several bolts were drawn back on the door, and my estimation of the neighbourhood reduced even further. Again, I found myself fighting the urge to run. But I stood there, and even managed a smile as the door was pulled open.

The face that appeared looked me up and down slowly. It frowned. I drew my hair back to reveal my scarred eye. It nodded, and the door was opened further.

The room beyond was small and packed with people. I hesitated.

"It's busy," I said. "I can't work with so many people here."

"Don't worry," the face said. "There's a bedroom beyond. It's completely private."

"I can't have too much noise."

"They'll be quiet, I promise. It's not a problem."

They placed a hand in the small of my back, and pushed me forward into the room. Everyone looked up at me, and stared.

"Perhaps..." I began, but the hand kept pushing me in. It pushed me through the group of people, that parted politely, or as politely as an intimidating crowd can, and pushed me right through the doorway into the bedroom. And then it shut the door.

Sat on the bed was a girl no older than myself. Her hands were pressed down between her thighs, and she looked up at me nervously. I glanced around. We were alone.

"Hi. I'm Kioto."

"I'm Ata."

"Is this your choice? Are you doing this because you want to?"

She nodded.

"Have you had an extraction before?"

She shook her head. "Well," she added. "Not since my Purification."

I nodded. It was a common ritual for citizens that involved the removal of the first four of five years of a child's memories. They claimed that it was to remove the trauma of the birth, first teeth, and so on, but I lived with those memories, and they didn't do any harm. The truth was, that to train as a trader or a merchant, you needed all of your memories intact. If even one was missing, you wouldn't ever be able to perform extractions. And citizens did not want their children to become merchants. The money could be good, but it was not something you hoped for your children. Traders and merchants did something invasive, something widely misunderstood, and so they were feared. And fear often masked itself behind hatred.

"Well, don't worry, it's not painful in the slightest. It feels a little bit odd, and can be uncomfortable as the memory comes out, but, believe me, this is a lot worse for me than it is for you."

Ata smiled slightly. "How come?"

"After performing an extraction, we suffer something called 'the throw'. It's nausea, dizziness, confusion, aching joints. A little bit like flu I suppose. Sometimes it's not too bad, other times you feel like you might die."

"Might you?"

"No, no, don't worry. No one's ever died from the throw."

Ata nodded again.

"Don't worry," I said. "It's going to be fine. Lie down and make yourself comfortable."

She lay back on the bed and shifted about for a while. As she finally stilled, I dropped my bag to the floor and opened it.

"Before we do the extraction, I'm going to perform the Dedication. It's just a traditional ceremony that traders do beforehand. I might say or do things that seem a little odd, but it's nothing to worry about. I'm simply calling the High in to assist me."

"Ok."

On the floor, I laid out my bowl, heather, rabbit pelt, and pebble. The bowl remained empty, it was only representative after all. The heather was brown and dry, and the pelt was matted and patchy. I ran my thumb over the pebble. It was chipped and cracked, but it was the only thing I had from Okaporo. I lifted it to my nose and breathed in the salty scent of it. In truth, it had probably lost its smell over the years, but my brain filled it back in.

I placed my fingers on the rim of the bowl, and closed my eyes. "My life was given by you, and will be offered up to you again. I will treasure your gift and use it in a way that glorifies your names."

I moved my hand to the prickle of the dried heather. "My roots were chosen by you, and your wisdom has set me on the correct path. I faithfully walk that path for you, and do so in your names."

I touched the pelt. "My family was given by you, and will be offered up to you again. They are my strength, my home, and my responsibility. I will love them in a way that honours your names."

I picked the pebble up into my hand. "You gave me free will, you gave me choices, and I will seek to mould my life with grace and truth. I will be influenced only by these things, and influence others by them. I choose to respect your teachings and follow your ways. For all of this I give thanks and ask for your blessing. Please stand with me as I perform this rite. Let my hands be your hands, my breath, your breath, and my heart, a vessel for your presence.

In your names, I ask this."

Standing, I turned around to the bed. I placed one hand on Ata's forehead, and the other on her stomach.

"Just relax," I whispered to her. "You'll feel me come into your mind. Don't panic, just invite me in. Then I want you to push forward the memory for extracting. Just think about it, and it will become obvious to me. Here we go."

Her mind resisted my presence at first. It nearly always happened, it was a reflex, a defence mechanism. But she relented and relaxed and, after a moment, a memory came forward.

I didn't run the memory, it wasn't mine to pry at. Some traders and merchants used the extraction like entertainment, like gossip. But it was none of my business what she wanted to forget. Or why. I collected the memory and deposited it deep in my mind.

I could feel the early beginnings of the throw already; a growing headache at the base of my skull. I pressed my eyes tightly closed and shook my head, but the movement exacerbated the pain. I was beginning to withdraw when another memory jumped in front of me.

"Do you want me to take this one as well?" I whispered. I felt Ata nod under my hand. "Are you sure?" She nodded again.

I tucked the memory away with the other, and withdrew from her mind.

"There, that wasn't too bad, was it?"

Ata began to sit up.

"Stay there for a moment," I said quickly. "You'll be a little dizzy, so just come up slowly. I have to get going, I need to get to a safehouse before the throw really kicks in."

I quickly packed my ritual items away, carefully tucking my pebble away into its separate pouch.

I gripped the edge of the bed and hauled myself up to standing, and a wave of nausea tried to bring me back to my knees.

"Can you see the memories you take from me?"

"If I look," I said, gulping down air. "But I choose not to."

"I think I'd be too curious. You can look at mine if you want to. It might help."

"Help what?"

"With the throw. I read that somewhere."

I snorted. I knew exactly where she'd read that. Several years ago, a trader called Sumi Cline had published a book—'The Secrets of The High'—in an attempt to increase understanding of colony traders, and improve the relationship between them and the rest of society. If anything, the book had served only to widen the rift. It did nothing to improve understanding, it merely laid the lives of colony traders bare for citizens to pick apart, belittle, and demonise. Sumi was despised on both sides.

"It's ok, I'm used to it," I said.

"I really don't mind. You can look at them. You should look at them."

The door opened then, and the person who had

opened the front door to me reappeared.

"All done?"

I nodded, my brain swimming.

"We'll sort out payment then. Have you got your cyber card?" He was playing it by the rules. By loading his payment onto the card, I'd have to return to the exchange to transfer it into my own account. Minus their commission charge, of course.

I took the cyber card back and pushed it into my pocket. There were large dark patches in my vision now, and I stumbled forward. I bashed my shoulder against something hard before a pair of hands stood me back up.

"You need to lie down," a voice said.

"I just need to get to a safehouse. I'll be fine."

"You're going nowhere in this state. Rest here, you'll be perfectly safe."

A sudden cramp across my stomach bent me double. I'd rarely experienced a throw this bad.

"I'll be fine," I said, but I didn't believe it. Trying to find a safehouse like this would be almost impossible, it was far more likely that I'd pass out in the street, and this wasn't the kind of neighbourhood you wanted that to happen in. I nodded, and allowed the hands to lead me to the bed.

"We'll just leave you to rest. You'll be fine."

"I hope you feel better soon," Ata said.

8

KIOTO

When I woke it was dark outside. I shivered. I didn't need to get up to know everyone had left, leaving behind a cold stillness.

I sat up slowly, testing my head. It was fogged with a dull aching, but it was otherwise fine. As I swung my legs around to sit on the edge of the bed, my foot caught in the strap of my bag. It was too light. Empty.

I looked down. Everything I owned was tossed across the floor. Or, at least, everything I owned that hadn't been of some value. I knelt down and gathered it up, cataloguing as I packed everything away. My knife was gone, and some of my clothes. My walking boots, my compass, a small statuette I'd traded for a while ago, my bag of herbs, my first aid kit, my solar lantern. And my pebble.

"Shit!" I screamed aloud.

I checked my pockets. Of course, they'd had no interest in my phone, it was a dinosaur, but the cyber card was gone. They'd taken back their payment.

With tears swelling in my throat, I swung my bag onto my back and stepped through to the living room. I'd been wrong. Not everyone had left. Ata was sat on the sofa.

"Where did they go?" I asked her.

"I'm so sorry," she said. "I didn't want to do it. They made me."

"Where did they go?"

"You shouldn't go after them. They're not safe. They'll hurt you."

I knotted my fists into my hair and screamed.

"I'm so sorry," Ata said again. "I tried to warn you."

"What? When?"

She tapped her temple.

"The memories," I whispered. Bringing them forward, I ran them through my head. The first one I'd taken was a memory of her being attacked. She was better off without that. The other showed Ata being forced into the plan to 'rip off a ripper'. She had tried to warn me. I nodded. "Thanks, I appreciate it."

"It was the only way I could think to tell you. Although, it probably would have been too late anyway."

"How come you stuck around?"

"I wanted to make sure you were ok. I honestly thought you were going to die."

"I appreciate it."

"You should get out of here, before they come back."

"Maybe you should too."

Ata shrugged. "I'll be alright."

"Really?"

She nodded. "Don't worry about me. Oh, did you want to give me my memories back? I know they're not good for you to hold onto."

"One of them I can sell. I can at least get something out of this horrible day. You can have your warning back. Maybe you can learn something from it. Stop letting those guys use you."

I pressed my hand against her forehead and pushed the memory back. It went easily; memories always wanted to be with their original host.

"I'm out of here," I said, and turned towards the door.

"Oh, this is yours," Ata said, holding up my pebble.

I snatched it from her open hand. "What have you got that for?"

She shrugged. "I thought it was pretty."

9

SENETSU

The sky above Okaporo was a smear of red in the dusk. It would have been beautiful if it wasn't accompanied by a breeze that carried the stench of death.

There was now nowhere to return to. We were officially lost. Refugees. Wanderers. It wasn't right for traders; our roots were important. But now, everything and everyone I ever knew was being burnt to dust. It was all just dust.

"What will Kioto return to?" I whispered. Saji didn't reply. "She's going to be so scared. Do you think Narata warned the rooks?"

"I'm sure she will have. Maybe they'll stay in Iwoyo with the children."

I frowned. "It's lucky they chose today to go."

"The High were looking after them. Narata was right; they are Okaporo's future now."

"Do you think Narata knew? That she sent the children away to save them?" I screwed my hands into fists. "Do you think she knew and said nothing until it was too late?"

The question hung in the darkness between us, and the consequences of its answer were too horrific to say aloud.

10

KIOTO

I folded my arms onto the counter of the exchange, and dropped my head into them. The screens on the back wall were blank and had been for some time. I'd tried to secure another two jobs, only to have them poached by merchants. At least, this time, the clients had been courteous enough to let me know before I'd arrived.

"Here," the woman behind the desk said, placing a mug of coffee and a sandwich in front of me.

I looked up at her with bleary eyes. "Thank you. So much."

"Not been a good day, has it?"

"Not at all," I replied, my mouth already full of bread.

"I wish I had something for you, but the network's gone silent."

"Thanks anyway." I picked up the coffee and turned around. It was beginning to get dark outside, and my good coat had been amongst the things they'd stolen. I needed somewhere to spend the night, but I didn't have enough money for a proper bed.

"Are there any safehouses nearby?"

"A couple. You want directions?"

I turned back to her and nodded. "Please."

She handed me a cyber card. "There's enough credit on there for a hot meal."

"Thank you. Again."

She smiled. "They're paid for by the colony. I give them to anyone who needs them. And they're needed more and more these days."

I smiled back at her. "Thanks. You've really looked after me today."

"I've been where you are."

I flicked the corner of the cyber card, and the first direction flashed up.

The safehouse was only a couple of streets away, fronted by a brightly lit café. It looked friendly, welcoming, but then, after the day I'd had, and with the growling ache in my stomach, anything would have looked welcoming.

I pushed the door open and stepped into the warm interior. It smelled of coffee, and cooked meat, and warm sugar. I pushed myself into a booth and grabbed the menu.

"I won't be a minute, love," called the waitress

from behind the counter. As she looked up, I spotted the scars over her eye. Looked like traders everywhere were having to find new streams of income.

My mouth watered as I looked over the menu, and I turned the cyber card over and over in my hand. It was the only good thing that had happened today.

My phone buzzed, and I pulled it from my pocket. As I did, another cyber card fell onto the seat beside me. I picked it up. It was the one the merchant had given me; directions to his off network contact. I laid the card on the table next to the one that would buy me a hot meal. One hot meal. Enough to get me through until tomorrow.

I looked at my phone. It was an automated message reminding me that my account was almost at its limit. Just what I needed.

I looked at the two cyber cards, side by side. One would fill my stomach for the night. The other would fill it for weeks. And it would buy that smudger. The one holding memories that belonged to my little sister.

"What can I get for you?" The waitress was suddenly by my side, and I scooped the merchant's card back into my pocket.

I held up the other card. "What does this get me?"

She cocked her head. "Anything you want, my love. Pudding too." She took it from me.

I smiled. "Pizza. And chips. And I'll have a

strawberry milkshake. And..." I flipped the menu over to the puddings. "Waffles and ice cream please."

"That's it, love, fill up your belly. Are you looking for a bed for the night too? We've only got a couple left, so say now if you want one."

"Yes, please."

"Not a problem." She patted me on the shoulder and disappeared into the kitchen beyond.

When I'd finished my meal, I leaned back and laced my hands over my very full stomach. I couldn't remember the last time I'd felt so full, and I didn't know when it might happen again.

I took out the other cyber card and turned it over in my hands. I could earn enough with this to buy the smudger and have enough left over for lots of meals. And a new coat and boots, better than the ones I had before. Off network jobs paid extremely well, but the punishments, if you were caught, were harsh. Even more so for a colony trader.

I tapped the card against the table. How else was I going to get 500 quickly enough? I couldn't let that merchant walk away with my sister's memories. Not when what I saw suggested that she could still be alive.

I didn't have a choice.

"I won't need that bed after all," I called back as I strode towards the door. If I didn't do this right now, I'd never do it. "Give it to someone else. And thank you."

11

KIOTO

I found myself standing outside a dentist's surgery. I looked down at the cyber card. This was definitely the address. It was just my luck that he'd moved on and now I had no bed for the night either.

I stepped forward and peered through the window into the dark interior, my hand cupped over my eyes.

The cyber card buzzed. I looked at it. One more direction. The arrow pointed down and to the right. Protruding from the corner of the building, was the end of a railing. I would never had spotted it.

As I rounded the corner, I saw that the railing marked a set of stairs leading down to a door. This was much more plausible.

Before knocking on the door, I checked the cyber card for instructions on some kind of secret knock. There weren't any. I grinned, and reminded myself that this was reality. So I lifted my hand and knocked as if I meant business. As if I'd called here a thousand times before and would be welcomed in as one of the family.

"No traders." The crackled voice came from a box on the wall.

"I was told to come here by Cota?" I offered.

"No traders."

"I'm not going away."

The box sighed. "Fine, come in, just don't expect a warm welcome."

"I'm used to that," I muttered as the door buzzed and I pushed it open.

The corridor beyond was dimly lit with red lights, the walls coated with paint of the same colour. It was like stepping inside a vein. A door at the far end stood ajar, and I made my way towards it.

"Hello?" I enquired, gently pushing the door a little further open.

"Well, come in if you're coming in," an impatient voice said.

I pushed the door open further and stepped inside.

A large desk took up the majority of the room, and sat behind it was a man who looked more like a toad then a man. His face disappeared into his neck, which disappeared into his shoulders, which, in turn, disappeared into his stomach. His head was mostly smooth, the expanse of skin interrupted only by the odd tuft of hair like marsh grasses. His eyes, enlarged by thick glasses, sat above a flat nose and a wide mouth.

The walls of the room were lined with shelves, and those shelves were crammed with artefacts. I spotted several traditional trader items, even some Arukumbi items, but most of them were unfamiliar. This man was clearly a collector. An appropriator of other cultures. I wondered how many of these items had been sacred to someone, and how much blood had been spilt to accumulate them.

His huge eyes scrutinised me. "How do you know Cota?"

"He poached a job from me."

The toad man huffed. "That, I can believe. He's no-nonsense when it comes to money, but he does have a soft spot for you folk and your funny ways."

"He said you might have some work for me."

"You people tend to avoid jobs like this. Too many scruples."

I shrugged. If I let him know I was desperate, the bargaining would swing very much in his favour. "I haven't belonged to a colony for a long time. I'm not exactly your traditional trader. I'm somewhat off network myself."

"An outcast. I meet a lot of those."

"So what do you have?"

"What are you willing to do?"

"Anything really. I'm saving up for a palace."

He snorted. "Then I might have something for

53

you. It pays big. 1200 on pick up, and another 1200 on delivery."

I attempted to bury the shock and excitement that tried to rush to my face. It could take me months to earn that with legitimate jobs.

I shrugged again. "That sounds alright."

"But it does require a deposit. Something I'll hold onto for now. Something precious." He stared hard at me. "Your pebble."

My heart went cold. "My pebble?" My voice came out as a squeak, confirming that he'd hit on the right item.

He tapped his glasses. "These see more than you know, and if there's one thing I know, it's people." He held out his hand.

"But I can't perform the Dedication without it."

"I'm sure that's not a problem for an 'off network' trader like you."

I swallowed hard. "When do I get it back?"

"After you complete the job."

"The extraction?"

He shook his head, sending ripples down to his stomach. "After delivery."

"I have to come back for it?"

He shook his head again. "I'll have it sent to the delivery point. It will be perfectly safe, I promise."

I wondered how much his promise was worth. Reluctantly, I dug into my bag and handed it over.

He weighed it in his hand for a moment. "Okaporo. That's tough. Anyway, here are the details." He tossed a cyber card at me. "When you arrive, show them that card. And I mean as soon as you arrive. This isn't somewhere you want to get mistaken as a trespasser. Understand?"

I waved a dismissive hand at him. "Not a problem."

12

KIOTO

The property was neither large, nor expensive looking, but it was well fortified. I found myself in front of tall metal gates topped with spikes. On the wall next to them was an intercom box. I glanced up at the camera watching me and held up the cyber card.

The intercom beeped, and an instruction popped up on the screen. INSERT CARD. I stepped forward and pushed the cyber card into the slot on the side. The instruction on the screen changed to READING. I waited. The intercom beeped again. ACCESS GRANTED.

The gates slid open, and I stepped through. The space beyond was functional and corporate, with nothing to indicate any kind of domesticity. The entire forecourt was tarmac, with not a single plant to break up the space. The building was square, squat, and unattractive.

I was met halfway across the forecourt by a woman running impressively fast in a pair of high heels. She linked her arm into mine and steered me towards one side of the building.

"Not in the front," she said.

I looked up at her. She had a long, sharp scar running along her jawline. It looked recent, but she hadn't tried to hide it. I could see that her make up stopped short of it, and her hair was tied back out of the way. Maybe she wanted to remind someone of it every time they looked at her.

"What's your name?" she asked.

"Kioto."

"We've been waiting a long time for you."

"I'm sorry, I have to walk. They never let my kind ride on the buses."

She waved her hand at me. "Sorry, that's not what I meant. I mean we specifically wanted a trader for this job, and it's been hard to find one willing. We're grateful to you."

"I see."

As we reached the building, a door was opened, and the woman led me through.

"Come on," she said. "We need to get started right away. Everyone's waiting for you."

She led me up a series of connecting corridors, down a set of stairs, up another, until I'd lost all sense of direction. I had no doubt that it was intentional.

We finally stopped at a door, and the woman knocked once before pushing it open. A merchant was standing in the room staring back at me.

"I don't believe this," I said. "I'm not losing another job to an egg." I turned to the woman. "We had an agreement. This is my job. Don't give it to a merchant." I lowered my voice. "Please, I need this."

"You never told me I'd be working with a red," the merchant complained.

"Ha!" I cried. "You're calling me a red? Yet you're here trying to poach an off network job from me."

"Calm down," the woman said, stepping between us. "No one's poaching your job," she said to me. "This job requires both of you." She turned to the merchant. "And if you don't want to work with a trader, Tian, then feel free to leave. There are loads of merchants who would be willing."

He muttered something I couldn't hear.

"No?" asked the woman. "Then keep your insults to yourself. Tian, meet Kioto. Kioto, this is Tian. There, now you know each other. You're both here for the same reason, because the money was too good to turn down. But if you can't work together, just say now, and I'll escort you out." Neither of us spoke. "Right then," she continued, "now we've got that out of the way, let's get down to business. Tian, you're up first. Follow me. Kioto, make yourself comfortable, I'll be back for you soon."

She led Tian back out of the door and closed it behind them.

I sat myself down on the plush sofa, folded my arms, and allowed myself to doze off.

I jumped as someone knocked on the door and then pushed it open. The woman gestured for me to follow her. She led me down a short corridor and into another room. A slave lay on a bed, watching me approach.

"Take the memory offered to you," the woman instructed. "Nothing else. No poking around, no prying. She'll tell me if you do." She gestured to the slave. "It's only a scratch, so even if you play it, it won't make any sense to you."

"Is it alright for me to perform the Dedication?" I asked.

The woman shrugged. "Whatever you need to do."

I laid out my altar items, minus the pebble of course. I glanced up at the woman, but she was looking away and hadn't noticed the omission.

I spoke quietly and quickly, performing the least reverent Dedication I ever had. I only hoped the High had had the time to hear it before it ended.

The memory was pushed through to my mind without hesitation, while everything else in her mind was held back from my reach. The slave was well-trained and knew what she was doing. She couldn't have been much more than fifteen years old, and I wondered how long she'd already been doing this for.

"Done," I said, stepping back.

"Let's get you settled before the throw kicks in,"

she said.

"I'd rather go to a safehouse," I replied.

"Absolutely not. We've got a room all set up for you. You'll be perfectly safe."

"I've heard that before," I mumbled.

13

KIOTO

The room had two beds, and the merchant, Tian, already occupied one. I lay down and turned my back to him.

"You don't have to act like a child," he said after a moment.

"I'll act however I like, thank you."

"How're you feeling?"

"Like I don't want to talk all the way through this."

"Fine." I heard him turn over in his bed. And then again. He fidgeted and shuffled about, and the bed squeaked under his constant motion.

"Are you completely incapable of keeping still?" I snapped.

"Are you completely incapable of keeping quiet? I'm trying to get some rest."

"And you usually sleep like that, do you? Like you're wrestling?" I rolled over and stared at him, the motion sending sharp pains through my skull.

He grinned at me annoyingly. "Maybe I do."

I grabbed my stomach as it churned and sloshed. "Is there a bathroom?" I mumbled.

Tian pointed to a door in the corner.

I only just made it to the toilet before I started retching, bringing up the only good meal I'd had in weeks. Such a waste.

"Would you like me to come and hold your hair back?" he called to me.

If I hadn't been hit with another bout of retching, he'd have received a very vicious response. How dare he not be as sick as me. How dare he be so frustratingly bright and healthy.

"You really are sick, aren't you?" He was at the bathroom door, watching my head disappearing into the toilet bowl.

"What do you care?"

His hand was on my back, rubbing it. "Because I'm a human, and you're a human, kind of, and I care about my fellow man. Or woman. Whatever."

I shrugged his hand off me. "I don't need any pity from someone like you."

"Then maybe I can give you an anti-sickness tablet. I've taken one. They work really well, trust me, my—"

"No," I said, cutting him off. "I don't need

anything from you. I have my ginger, and my chamomile." I groaned as I remembered that they'd been stolen. "I did. Shit."

"Well, the offer's still open. There's no point in suffering needlessly. Do you always get the throw so badly?"

I turned around and looked up at him, my stomach churning a little less for now.

"No. It must be something else making me nauseous. Or someone."

He placed his hand on his heart in a mock show of hurt. "Vicious, aren't we? Are you always so rude to people you've only just met?"

"Must we do this? I feel like crap and you suddenly want to mend generations of burnt bridges between your kind and mine?"

"I'm not trying to mend anything between my kind and yours. Just me and you. I shouldn't have called you a red when we first met, you just kind of surprised me. I'm sure you have a good reason for taking an illegal job, just like I do. Anyway, we're going to be here for a while, you're in pain, and I can help to ease that. If you swallow your pride and let me."

"It has nothing to do with pride. I just don't trust taking medicine from a merchant."

He rolled his eyes. "Fine. Suffer. See if I care." He went back and lay down on his bed.

Slowly, carefully, I dragged myself to my feet. I shuffled to the door and clung onto the door frame. "See," I said. "I'm feeling better already."

"Yeah, you look great."

"Are you going to sulk now?"

He stuck out his bottom lip. "What do you care?"

I held up my hands. "Whatever. I'm done. I'm going to get some sleep, so you can just talk to yourself."

"Luckily, I'm really good company."

"Well, that's good then." I stumbled to the bed and dropped onto it, tugging the cover over myself just as I started to shiver. I reached my arm down and pulled my bag under the cover with me, cuddling into it.

I closed my eyes and groaned. My head was spinning, which was not helping my stomach to settle. To make it worse, the new memory was sat like a thorn in my brain. I groaned again.

"Are you alright?" Tian whispered.

"Yes." I whispered back.

"You're clearly not."

"It's just hard to sleep with a scratch in my head."

"Partial memories aren't comfy at all, are they? I guess that's why they call them scratches."

"Doh, yeah, really?"

I heard him shift from his bed, and then my cover lifted up, and suddenly he was in my bed, just lying next to me casually like we did this everyday.

I twisted round to look at him. "What do you think you're doing?" I said, still whispering.

"You looked like you needed some company."

"And how could you tell that when I had my back

to you?"

"Maybe it was your tone of voice then."

"That tone was sarcasm."

"Doh, yeah, really?" he said.

"Get out of my bed."

"Fine. Fine." He backed up and sat on the edge of his own bed. "I'm sorry it's so awful having to spend some time with me."

"I'm not spending time with you. I'm trying to spend time with myself, and you keep interrupting."

"Do you want me to be quiet?"

"That's all I want."

"Me to be quiet."

"Yes."

The door to the room was flung open, slamming against the chest of drawers beside it.

"Feeling better?" It was a man this time, his face barely discernible behind a wiry veil of facial hair.

"Not really," I grumbled.

"Well, it's time for you to leave. Let's say you've officially outstayed your welcome."

"That didn't take long," said Tian.

"Far too long if you ask me," I said. I clambered from the bed and hefted my bag onto my back. I took the cyber card the man offered to me, and Tian took his.

"Your first half of the payment is loaded onto the card, fully unlocked, so you can use that whenever. The second half of it is locked, and will be made available in Honporo. You must travel separately but," the man looked at me, "I'm sure that won't be a problem. You have two weeks to deliver."

"Two weeks? It will only take a couple of days to get to Honporo."

"For you, maybe. But not everyone can travel in luxury." The man glared at me again. "We have to make allowances for that."

"C'mon," Tian said, "you can give her a lift, can't you? You can't expect her to walk all that way."

The man jabbed a finger towards Tian, then at me. "Do not travel together. And watch your backs. We wouldn't want anything happening to you."

I looked down at the cyber card, the first direction already flashing. Honporo. I hadn't been back to the coast since Okaporo. Hadn't seen, or even smelt the sea. Just the thought of it brought back the stench of death.

14

KIOTO

"I bet you were surprised to hear from me again," I said as I approached Cota.

He shook his head. "Not really. I knew you wouldn't be able to resist it. Once people have temptation in their hands, they can't help but imagine giving into it. And once you start imagining it, the deal's already done."

"You have a pretty low opinion of people."

He shrugged. "So, you still want my smudger?"

"Is there any room for negotiation on that price?"

"500. Take it or leave it."

"Fine."

Cota lifted his fingers and drew out a screen in the air between us. I pulled out my cyber card and waved it close to the screen.

"That's not how you do it," Cota said, snatching the card from me. He touched the card to the screen and it beeped. Payment accepted. It was nice not to hear the double beep again, and even nicer knowing that it would be some time before I did.

He closed his fingers and thumbs together and the screen fizzled and vanished. He waggled his fingers at me. "You should invest in some implants, join the rest of this century."

"No thank you."

Cota opened the back of his wagon and dragged the smudger out. Her hands were chained together.

I sighed. "You can take those off," I said.

"You might want to keep them on," Cota replied. He dropped a small key into my hand.

"Where are her papers?"

Cota grinned. "I lost them."

"You can't sell a carrier without papers."

"And who are you going to complain to? Besides, look at her, she's got the shivers so bad she'll be dead within weeks."

"I can't go round with a carrier without documents. Especially one in this state. What if we get stopped?"

"Well, you'd better avoid the authorities then. I'm sure that's like second nature to you."

"Great. Thanks. That's really helpful."

He climbed up into the front of his wagon. "Enjoy your smudger while you still have her." He swung the door closed and the engine hummed. The wagon pulled away, and we watched it leave.

"Bye bye, bye bye," the smudger said.

"I'm Kioto. What's your name?"

"I don't know, I don't know."

"That's ok, we'll figure it out."

"What's your name?"

"Kioto."

"What's your name?" she repeated.

"Let's get those chains off you. You're free now." I unlocked them and dropped them into my bag. The smudger looked at her hands for a while, turning them over and over.

"I'm just going to have a quick look inside your head, if that's alright. I'll be gentle."

I reached my hand up to her forehead and she shied away. Being a carrier, enslaved, was bad enough, but when you were designated as the smudger, forced to carry all the bad, unhappy, violent memories, when it came, death was a welcome release.

I rubbed her arm. "It's ok, I just want to look, I'm not going to put anything in, I promise. You're safe now."

She held still this time, but her eyes flicked from side to side with panic. She was full, her brain almost bursting with horrible memories she had been forced to take. There was no way I could extract any, no way that I could even look through them to find more of my sister's. Any prodding could cause a rush; a sudden and uncontrollable emptying of her head into mine. It would be enough to kill me outright. It was a

69

miracle that she was still alive.

"We'll get you sorted, alright? When we get to Honporo we'll go to the colony and get some help. But now, we've got a long walk ahead of us. A very long walk."

15

SENETSU

I passed Omori from my arms into Saji's. He shifted her weight, her head lolling against his neck.

"Thank you," I said. "She was getting so heavy."

"She's exhausted. As are you."

"I know. But we have to keep moving."

"No," Saji said, touching my arm. "No. Enough. No more walking all day long. No more sleeping in barns and caves and makeshift shelters. You and Omori have barely slept at all."

"She's having nightmares. About Okaporo, and about Kioto. When she asks me where her sister is, or when we'll see her again, what can I say? I don't know. And then she thinks about all the possibilities, and by bedtime they've become nightmares in her head."

"Exactly. You both need a proper rest. If we head that way, we can make it to Akimori before nightfall."

"And what are we going to do in Akimori?"

"Rest. Recharge. Just for a couple of days. Wouldn't it be nice to wake up tomorrow morning and know that you don't have to walk anywhere?"

"That would be so nice."

"And to sleep in a real bed. Have a bath. Eat a proper meal."

I was already imagining sinking into the water, hot enough to turn my skin red.

"We could stop at the colony there."

"No. No colony. No bunking on mats. And no safehouses either; sleeping in a dormitory, and probably only getting one bed between us, sharing with traders recovering from the throw. No. We deserve a little bit of luxury."

"But we've barely got any money. We've almost emptied our accounts, and we've already sold our rings. Any work we've done along the way was just traded for food."

"We've got enough left."

"But it will wipe us out completely. What if there's an emergency?"

Saji shifted Omori's body to his other hip. She lifted her head for a moment, but quickly dropped it down and went back to sleep.

"I don't know about you, but I'd call this an emergency."

I smiled. "When you put it that way."

"Good. Decision made."

We purposefully avoided the colony at Akimori, and entered the city through the suburbs. We were stared at, pointed at, and a few insults were thrown our way, but it was nothing we hadn't experienced before.

I gripped Omori's hand tightly as she trundled along beside me. I couldn't protect her from it, all I could do was reassure her. So we set our focus on the pavement ahead and walked with our heads held high. And our four year old daughter copied. Our four year old daughter learnt how much she was hated, and how to pretend it wasn't happening.

We walked right into the centre of the city, where auto-cars hummed past us, their passengers relaxed in the climate-controlled, leather interiors.

The streets here were packed with people, and we were barely even noticed. No one stopped to stare, no one pointed. We were invisible.

We passed several hotels and guest houses that prominently displayed signs stating NO TRADERS. We knocked on the doors of some that didn't, only to be met with the rebuffal in person, or a claim of "no vacancies".

We didn't even make it to the front door of one.

"No, no, no, no, no!" The woman came running out waving her hands, her feet still in her slippers. "Not you. Not your kind." Her eyes had fallen on Omori then, and for a moment, I thought she might reconsider, but then her eyes snapped back to my face, or, more specifically, my right eye. "No, get out of here, you're not welcome."

She muttered something as we turned around, but I was too tired to listen for what it was.

"This is useless," I said to Saji. "So much for that hot bath."

"I'm sorry, I shouldn't have even suggested it. Maybe we should head for the colony after all."

Omori was walking slower and slower, her head beginning to droop.

"I think that's a good idea," I said. I bent and lifted her up onto my hip.

"Mummy," she whispered into my neck. "When are we going home?"

"We're not, darling."

"Is Kioto at our old home or our new home?"

"I don't know where Kioto is," I replied tightly.

"Why don't people want us to sleep in their houses?"

For a moment I considered lying to her, telling her that they simply had no room for us. But it was the rest of the world that was the problem, not us. There was nothing wrong with us, and I never wanted Omori to think that there was. Not even for a moment.

"Because they don't like people who are different to them."

"Are we different?"

"They think we are."

"Why?"

"Because we don't live in their big houses, and we don't do the same jobs as them, and because we believe in different things."

"Like what?"

"Like the High."

She sat up in my arms. "They don't believe in the High?"

"No, darling."

"But you know what that means," she whispered.

"People choose to believe different things, and that's fine, that's their choice, isn't it? Now, we know that the world is a wonderful place because everyone in it is different. Remember Matsu from back home? Remember her beautiful red hair? Well, imagine if there were no red haired people in the world. Wouldn't that be sad?"

"There's no Matsu?"

The question hit me like a spear through my chest. There probably was no Matsu anymore.

"I mean, imagine if she had black hair instead. If everyone had black hair. It would be sad to never see red hair again, or blonde, or white, or all the other colours."

"It would be sad."

"And that's why it's good that the world is full of different people."

"But they don't like different?"

"Some people are afraid of different."

"That's silly."

"You're right, it's very silly. Which is why we don't get angry when people treat us badly. Because it's just them being silly, and there's no point getting angry over that, is there?"

Omori shook her head. "Sometimes silly is fun."

I tickled her ribs and she squirmed. "Sometimes silly is fun."

"Look," said Saji, tugging on my arm.

I looked at the house where he was pointing. I blinked and looked again. The sign in the window stated TRADERS WELCOME.

"Maybe not everyone in this city is afraid of different," I said.

Saji pushed open the gate, and we walked up the short path.

16

SENETSU

I leaned back in the bath and closed my eyes. The bubbly water steamed, and my insides gently cooked. Omori was tucked up in a bed of her own, and we had a locked door between us and the rest of the world. It's surprising how much you miss that when you don't have it.

For the first time since leaving Okaporo, Omori was sleeping soundly. She wasn't crying and fighting, she wasn't screaming out Kioto's name as she slept. For once, she hadn't sobbed herself into an exhausted sleep. She felt safe and secure, and it showed.

Saji was watching the television, the sound turned too low for me to hear what was on. We'd had a small one in Okaporo, but it rarely got plugged in. It showed little more than back to back adverts these days, for things that, even if we could afford them, no one would ever sell to a trader anyway. It was a constant reminder that we were outsiders. And so, we'd simply unplugged it.

I dropped my face under the surface of the water and listened to it swirl around me. I could stay here forever, happily pretending that the outside world didn't exist, but we'd only had enough money for two nights. Saji had been right, though; it was enough time to simply recharge and catch up on our sleep. Then we would set out for Kumonayo, which was at least another three days' hike. We'd have to make the most of this while we could.

"Senetsu!" Saji called. "Okaporo's on the TV!"

I jumped out of the bath and stumbled through to the bedroom, tripping on the towel as I tried to wrap it around myself. I sat on the edge of the bed and stared.

The images showed our burnt out homes, the scorched ground beneath them. They were saying that they'd found dozens of bodies, but they had been too burnt to identify.

I'd done my own crying; spent days in tears, cried myself to sleep every night. Tears rolled down my cheeks again, but they weren't for the home I'd lost, or the people I'd known this time, it was seeing what Kioto would have seen when she thought she was coming home.

"Are they only just reporting this now?" I asked. It had happened almost two weeks ago.

"I'm amazed they're covering it at all. There's clearly not much else going on."

And then the images were gone, replaced by some kind of première or opening. People didn't want to know about dead traders when they could check out the latest fashions their favourite movie stars were wearing.

"Sorry to drag you from your bath," Saji said. He put his arm around me and pulled me up against him, despite my wet hair and skin.

"It's fine."

"Are you getting back in?"

"I think I'd rather just go to bed," I said.

We slept in until almost eleven the next morning, running downstairs to the breakfast room full of apologies. But the landlady, Mrs Rido, wouldn't hear any of it.

"You needed that sleep, especially the little one, and you all look a lot better for it. Now, what can I get you for breakfast?"

"We're not too late?" Saji asked.

"What's late? Come on, what do you fancy?"

We ate until our bellies ached, and our eyelids started to droop again.

"What are your plans for the day?" Mrs Rido asked.

"We really don't have any," replied Saji, "which is, actually, exactly what the plan was."

"A day of relaxation, eh? Sounds like a good idea. In which case, why don't you move into our guest lounge? There's toys and books and a TV."

"Sounds good," I said, glancing at Omori. She was already jiggling up and down in her seat.

As we left the breakfast room, Mrs Rido caught my arm. "I noticed that you didn't arrive here with any luggage at all, and, you look like you've done your absolute best with them, but I'm sure you could all do with some clean clothes. I collect donations for charity. Why don't you come and take a look. You can grab a few outfits for all of you."

"No, no, we couldn't possibly—"

"Nonsense," she said. "I won't take 'no' for an answer. Come on."

She led me to a cupboard which was jammed with all the essentials; clothes, shoes, bags, toys, toiletries.

"Take whatever you want," Mrs Rido said. "And don't be polite, or modest. Everyone needs more than one outfit, and you certainly need a good coat for that girl of yours. And you need some better boots. So help yourself, and if you don't take enough, I won't let you leave until I've forced more onto you. There's plenty of rucksacks there, so fill a couple of those." She smiled and patted my shoulder.

"Thank you, so much. Seriously, no one is ever this kind to traders."

"At the end of the day, we're all human, and we both want the same thing: for that little girl to be safe, and warm, and happy. Those eyes of hers just melt your heart, don't they."

"Well, thank you. This is more than generous."

"I'll leave you to it. Take whatever you want."

I didn't hold back. I took every cold stare, every pointed finger, every insult we'd suffered in Akimori, and I pushed it into my hands as I furiously rummaged. I dug out warm, practical clothes, thick pyjamas, warm socks, underwear, sturdy boots. I grabbed toothbrushes, toothpaste, deodorants, sanitary pads. All the things we always took for granted, and all the things we'd been living without. I took razors, and toys, and toilet paper, and plates, and mugs, and cutlery. Blankets, sleeping bags, pillows. I crammed them into the two biggest rucksacks I could find, and then I filled every side pocket, and even tied items to the straps.

We only had three more days of walking in front of us, but we'd be arriving in Kumonayo with nothing, and we'd have to create a home from nothing, and I didn't want to arrive there with my begging bowl in hand. I didn't want their pity, or their sympathy, because if I saw sorrow in their faces, I wouldn't be able to contain mine. I needed to make something familiar in a strange place, give Omori somewhere to feel safe. I couldn't do that if I was falling apart, and I couldn't burden Saji with the responsibility of being strong for the both of us. He'd lost just as much as I had.

17

KIOTO

I sat and watched the smudger sleep for a while. She was kicking and twitching, crying out, her eyes roved under her eyelids. I wondered when she'd last had a peaceful night's sleep.

I pushed her matted hair back from her damp face. Her skin was so pale, and her features were so Arukumbi that you could never mistake her for anything else.

Her people had been persecuted, tortured, killed, and enslaved for hundreds of years, since the Lobayans first invaded. If colony traders were kept at arm's length, the Arukumbi had been kept at the end of a spear. The suffering of my people was nothing in comparison.

They hadn't been allowed to mix with Lobayans, and as a result, their culture had stayed intact, albeit hidden away. Modern day Lobayans, on the other hand, were little more than mongrels. There were stories and theories about where colony traders had come from, but no one theory pushed itself to the fore with evidence. It was as if we'd simply sprung from the ground one day. It was sad to know so little about my own ancestry when I could happily rattle off a hundred facts and dates about the Arukumbi.

The rooks in the colonies liked to teach about Arukumbi history. It served several agendas: to keep the Arukumbi history alive as a rebellious act against the authorities (the enemy of my enemy is my friend and all that), it showed young traders that they weren't the only persecuted people, and it also showed them that there were people who had it worse than they did.

We'd found some abandoned properties on the edge of Miyakata, almost overlooking the colony there. The broken windows provided easy access, and judging by the mattresses and empty food and drink containers, we weren't the first people to make use of them.

I wandered to the window and glanced up at the dark sky. It was overcast, so there were no stars to be seen. I silently recited the Grace. I'm sure the High would understand that the thought of completing the full ceremony, minus my pebble, was not an enticing prospect. After reciting the words I'd said every day of my life since I was able, I added a promise to complete the full ceremony tomorrow.

The smudger seemed a little more settled, so I lay down on a mattress next to her and closed my eyes. Not that I expected to get much sleep. The scratch was digging into my brain. It was like trying to sleep with your head on a rock.

It was already light when I woke. I'd hoped to get away at first light, but the sun was already high above the buildings. I shrugged, I'd obviously needed the rest. Besides, the walk from Miyakata was eight or nine days at best, we could afford a lie in.

I looked over at the smudger. She was lying with her back to me, breathing deeply. I wasn't going to interrupt her while she was actually quiet.

I took the time to go through my bag; work out what I needed to replace and what I could live without.

I looked up as the smudger rolled over. Her face was covered with blood. I sat and stared for a second, my brain taking a moment to catch up.

I crawled over to her and took hold of her face in my hands. She opened her eyes and blinked as they filled with blood.

"You're alright, you're alright," I said. "You've hurt yourself, but we'll get you some help. Ok?"

She nodded, her eyes focused on mine. Completely focused. No sign of the shivers.

"What's your name?" I asked her.

"Malia."

"I'm Kioto."

"You told me yesterday."

"I did. I wasn't sure if you... if you'd remember."

"What's happened to me?" she asked, looking at her blood covered hands.

"I don't know. I guess you bashed your face on the floor. We need to get you to a hospital. Do you think you can walk?"

She nodded.

"But let's get you cleaned up first. I doubt there's any running water here, and I've not got a first aid kit anymore, but I can wipe you down as best I can. Is that alright, if I do that?"

She nodded slowly.

"I'll be gentle, I promise."

I pulled a shirt from my bag and gently wiped her face down. I cleaned her hands as best I could. I could see where the blood was coming from now; her forehead was completely split open, and she had a number of deep scratches around her eyes.

"There was a lot of blood. It looked worse than it is. But we need to get you stitched up. Come on. We'll go slowly, and if you need to stop at any time, just tell me. It doesn't matter if it takes us all day to get there."

We found our way to the hospital with ease—it was clearly signposted far out from the city centre—but we stopped many times for Malia to rest. She was dizzy, and as we walked, her shivers returned and she twitched, and called out, and made less and less sense. And she no longer seemed to hear me, or, at least, didn't seem to comprehend what I was saying.

By the time we reached the hospital, her shivers were convulsing her whole body and I was worried that it might cause her to start bleeding again.

I stared at the front doors of the hospital. It was busy, with a constant stream of people going in and out. Ambulances hummed past us, taxis, buses. And there were officers here too. Lots of officers. I looked at Malia. I didn't have a choice. We started to walk towards the building.

I jumped as someone grabbed hold of my arm, and span round to face Tian.

"What are you doing here?" I asked.

"You're not taking her in, are you?" he said.

I gestured to her bloodied face. "Yeah, I was thinking about it."

He placed his arm around my shoulders and turned me around. I grabbed hold of Malia and she trailed along beside us as Tian led us away.

"She needs medical attention," I said.

"I know. But you can't take her in there. Even I can see she's got the shivers, and badly by the looks of it. They'll take her away from you. Do you even have papers for her?"

I shook my head.

"Then you'll end up in jail too."

"So what do I do? Look at her."

"I'll sort her. But first, we need to find somewhere we can have some privacy. You can't just walk around the streets with a topped out smudger with no documents."

We had no choice but to head for a safehouse;

even if we'd found somewhere that would rent a room to a trader, there's no way they would have let Malia in in her state.

Safehouses didn't tend to ask questions, and they didn't tend to turn anyone away, especially when they made a substantial 'donation'. We even managed to get a private room.

"How much did you bribe him?" I whispered to Tian.

"You don't want to know."

"I'll pay you back."

Tian waved a hand at me. "My treat."

"I insist."

"Just get her as comfortable as you can, and I'm going to go get some medical supplies. Lock the door behind me. Don't go anywhere, and don't let anyone in that door. Let's just hope no one reports us."

I locked the door as he'd instructed, and lay Malia down in one of the beds. I lay next to her and stroked her hair.

"He'll be back soon," I said. "Then we'll get you better."

"He'll be back," Malia repeated.

Her eyes were beginning to droop, so I slipped off the bed and left her to rest.

Underneath the window was a small bookcase and I crouched down to browse the titles. There were several books on Arukumbi history, some herbology books, and various books about the art of memory trading: 'Finding Peace with Other People's Memories', 'More Art Than Science', 'Extracting

Memories from Children' (a practice that wasn't exactly banned in the colonies, but very much discouraged). There was even a book called 'Extracting Memories from Animals'. I smiled. Some people were insane. Turned around to display its pages rather than its spine was a copy of 'The Secrets of the High'. I flicked it open. It had been violently defaced, with almost every page scrawled with corrections, or insults, or juvenile sexual images. So much for non-censorship of the arts. I put it back as I had found it.

Someone knocked on the door, and I spun around.

"It's me," came Tian's voice. "Let me in."

He came in with a full bag, a pharmacy logo printed on the side.

"How much did that cost?" I asked. "I will definitely pay you back for that."

"Then your debt's already settled, because I got it all for free." He flashed me a smile.

He crossed to the bed and placed a hand on Malia's shoulder. She rolled over onto her back and looked up at him.

"How are you feeling?" he asked her.

"He'll be back," Malia said, reaching up to touch Tian's face.

"That's right. I'm back. So let's get you all fixed up."

Tian worked in silence, biting his bottom lip with concentration throughout. Malia sat relatively calmly, but she was unable to control her twitching and occasional vocal outbursts. Tian, however, treated her with such gentleness and patience, and showed no sign of being annoyed by her inability to keep still.

"All done," he said, turning her around to face me. The gash in her forehead had been expertly sewn and taped, the scratches had been rubbed with cream, and the bigger ones taped across. She wouldn't have been treated any better if I had taken her to the hospital. He handed her a glass of water. "Drink that and have a lie down. You need to get some sleep. Let your body heal." He tucked her under the covers and smoothed her hair back from her face.

18

SENETSU

Sitting in possibly the most comfortable armchair I'd ever sat in, I spent most of the morning dozing in and out of sleep. We'd spent every day walking for so long now that my body simply didn't know what else to do with this stillness.

Omori divided her time between playing and watching TV, and Saji seemed to have completely disappeared into a romance novel. I'd never known him read fiction before, and I smiled at his surprising immersion into it.

"I need to get up," I said. "If I sit here any longer I'm actually going to become part of this chair."

I stretched, my shoulders and back cracking in several places.

"You really did need to move," Saji said.

"Or I'm just getting old."

He pointed a finger at me. "Just remember that I didn't say that."

Mrs Rido appeared in the doorway. "Look at the three of you. So relaxed and well-rested."

"Yes, it was exactly what we needed," I said.

"Would you like some lunch, or do you have other plans?"

"We only paid for bed and breakfast," Saji said.

She waved her hands at us. "Never mind that. It's nothing fancy anyway, just soup and sandwiches, but there's far too much for just me, so you're more than welcome to some.

I cocked my head at Saji.

"Yes, thank you, that would be lovely," he said.

"I'll call you when it's ready. Around ten minutes if that's alright?"

"That's perfect, thank you," I replied.

Mrs Rido nodded and disappeared.

"Isn't that nice of her?" I said, turning to Saji.

"Really nice of her. And to think we could've ended up in a stinky safehouse."

"Or bedding down in another barn."

Saji groaned. "Anything but that. I don't think I can stand another night breathing in the stench of cows."

I spluttered with laughter. "Remember that time you woke up to one chewing your hair?"

Saji laughed. "And I remember the day that little boy walked in and saw us sleeping there. Remember?

I've never heard a child scream so loud."

"No wonder his father came running with his gun already loaded. He must've thought we were killing the lad."

"Even when he saw us I don't think it eased his panic any."

"No, I'm surprised we didn't end up with bullets in our buttocks." I grinned. "Y'know, I'm absolutely starving now we're thinking about lunch."

"Mmmm, me too."

"Me three," said Omori.

"Have you had a nice day so far?" I asked, crouching down to her.

She nodded hesitantly. "I wish Kioto was here."

I sighed. "Mrs Rido's nice, isn't she?"

She nodded again, her curls bouncing. "Is Kioto coming to play? Is she still in bed?"

"Kioto's not here." I looked up at Saji. "I'm just going to the bathroom."

He nodded and picked his book back up.

As I stepped out into the hallway I could smell lunch, and my stomach rumbled impatiently. The small downstairs toilet was like the rest of the guest house; tidy, clean, sweet smelling, and decorated with frills, lace, and flowers. It was all a little old fashioned, but in a cosy, homely way, not a garish one.

As I came out and headed back towards the guest lounge, Mrs Rido intercepted me.

"Oh, is lunch ready?" I asked her.

"Very soon, dear, very soon. I just wanted to talk to you about your daughter first. She's enjoyed it here, hasn't she?"

"Yes, she has."

"Enjoyed the toys, the bed. Enjoyed the rest, I'll bet. And having a bit of stability. Children need stability, don't they? Somewhere they know is safe, a home that they know will always be there."

"Yes, that's what we want for her. And once we get to—"

"Life on the road is no life for a little one," Mrs Rido interjected. "And I know you want the very best life for her that you can. That's what any mother wants."

"Yes, of course—"

"And that's a life that she can have, right here in Akimori."

"We're not staying in—"

"Now, I'm sure you've heard a lot of horror stories about the Liberation Scheme, but it really is a very positive thing for the children."

I instinctively backed away, but found my heels against the skirting board in just a few steps.

"They will have a stable home. No more travelling, no more uncertainty, no more living as outcasts. Your little one will benefit from a proper education, proper access to healthcare, and a good, clean, secure home. Isn't that all we want for our children?"

"Saji!" I called out.

"You'd be doing the best for her, and you'd be able to take comfort in that knowledge."

"Saji!" I screamed. I saw his head emerge from

the guest lounge past Mrs Rido. "Liberation!" I shouted.

Mrs Rido grabbed hold of my wrist, her grip like that of a gorilla.

"You know it's the only choice." Her face was up into mine, her eyes ablaze with intensity. "I have officers on their way to collect her, you won't get away. They're already outside."

"Let go!" I screamed, wrenching my arm free. I shoved her, hard, as I ran past, and I didn't look back. I grabbed the bags I'd filled earlier from inside the door of the guest lounge, and followed Saji and Omori out of the front door.

"We need to go, now!" I yelled.

Saji lifted Omori into his arms and ran. I followed, with both bags bouncing against my back. I didn't know if there really were officers on their way, but we weren't going to be here to find out.

19

KIOTO

"I've never seen her sleep so soundly," I said.

Tian grinned. "I slipped her a couple of sleeping pills."

"Good thinking. Bless her, I can't even imagine how awful an existence that must be."

"Yeah, right. It's bad enough living with your own bad memories, let alone everyone else's." He was quiet for a moment. "What do you want her for anyway?"

"That's none of your business," I snapped.

He held his hands up defensively.

"You're right, it's none of my business. I was just curious."

"Where did you learn to do that, anyway?" I

asked, gesturing towards Malia.

"My dad's a doctor, well, a consultant," Tian replied. "That's why I was at the hospital yesterday. I was going to be a doctor too. Did a few years of medical school before dropping out."

"And becoming a memory merchant? Bet your dad was really proud of you."

Tian smiled grimly. "Practically disowned me. I mean, I still live in his house, but we barely speak, and when we do, it's more like forced politeness."

"How on earth does someone go from training to be a doctor, following in their father's footsteps, to dropping out of society's approval to become a merchant?"

"Well, you may not believe it, but my mum was actually a colony trader."

I turned around on the bed to face him. "Really?"

He nodded. "Yep. My grandparents still are. They tried to teach me all the old, traditional stuff, but I wasn't a very good student. I was too interested in modern life. Modern life, friends, going out. Girls. But they must have inspired me somehow."

"What about your mum? Is she still a trader?"

"She's dead."

I felt my face flush. "Oh, I'm sorry."

He shrugged. "It's ok, it happened when I was really young. She'd already left the colony, and was practising as a merchant, but her scars," he raised his hand to his eye, "marked her out. She was beaten to death on the streets one night. I was four years old. My father and grandparents raised me."

I laid my hand over my heart. "My heart aches for you." The standard response was out of my mouth before I could stop it. "I'm sorry. Old habits..."

"That's ok."

"It's not though. I really mean it, I'm sorry, and spouting some canned response doesn't convey any kind of sorrow or sincerity."

"Why do you guys do that?"

"Make up standard responses to things?" I thought for a moment. "I dunno. Maybe so many bad things have happened to traders over the centuries that it just became an easier way to deal with it."

Tian nodded and looked down at his hands in his lap.

"So what made you take on a job like this?" I asked. "Or is this all in a day's work for you?"

"Wow, no. I guess... I just couldn't turn it down. I really needed the money."

I laughed. "Yeah, sure."

"No, really. Remember I said my father practically disowned me? He tolerates my presence out of a sense of duty, but I really need to get a place of my own. Trouble is, they don't come cheap. I don't want to rely on him for anything. And the last thing I want is to end up like him; bitter, alone, miserable. If I stay living with him, I'm afraid that's the inevitable outcome. I'd die before I ended up like him."

"I can't understand how he can treat you with such flippancy, after he raised you alone, after he lost his wife—"

"They weren't married, my mum and dad. They

weren't really even a couple. Their relationship was on and off for years. Sometimes mum actually lived with dad, but, according to my grandparents, she could never stand it for too long, and kept running back to the colony. I get the feeling that it was never particularly serious between them. Just familiar and comfortable, I guess."

I nodded slowly, not sure what to say next. The silence hung between us for a moment, angular and uncomfortable.

"What made you take the job?" Tian finally asked.

I glanced over at Malia. "I needed the money."

"How much did you pay for her?"

I rolled my eyes. "500."

"Wow, someone saw you coming."

I shrugged. "I think she'll be worth it."

"But you're not going to tell me what for."

I shook my head. It wasn't something I dared to say out loud, in case I'd been mistaken, in case I, somehow, made it untrue simply by telling someone else.

"So how would your brood mother deal with you taking on ripped jobs like this?"

"I don't have a brood mother."

"Which colony do you belong to?"

I shook my head. "None."

"A rogue?"

"Definitely not," I snapped.

Tian held his hands up. "Ok, touchy subject. Is there a subject with you that isn't touchy or clandestine?"

I dropped back onto the bed and laced my hands behind my head. "What would you like to talk about? My tragic past? My hellish childhood? My abandonment issues?"

"Alright, alright, we'll avoid talking about anything to do with you then."

I rolled over onto my side and looked up at him. "Have you ever thought about joining a colony?"

He laughed. "I like my creature comforts too much. I'm just not designed for roughing it."

"I guess it's all I've ever known."

"Have you ever thought about leaving it all behind?"

"For what? What else is there for me?" I pushed back my hair to show my scars. "The world will only ever see these three lines. I'll never be anything else. You know that well enough."

Tian nodded. "I guess I do."

20

KIOTO

We left Miyakata at first light, stopping off for supplies, and then walking out through the suburbs before the rest of the world woke up. It was the only time to do it; a trader with a carrier and a merchant trailing behind them would have brought far too much attention.

I turned around as we left the last few buildings of Miyakata behind us.

"Aren't you going to catch a bus, or something?" I called to Tian.

"Nope. It's a nice day, I fancy the walk."

I looked up at the heavy clouds above us. The wind was already damp, and rain wasn't far off.

"Yeah, lovely," I said. "If you're going to walk, can

you at least come and walk with us, instead of trailing behind like you're stalking us?"

"No can do," he replied with a grin. "We're not meant to travel together, remember?"

"I can't have you walking behind us like that. It's making me nervous."

"Me too," said Malia with a giggle. I looked at her. It was the first time I'd seen her smile.

"How's your head feeling today?" I asked her.

She touched the bandages with her fingertips. "Much better. He did a good job."

"He did, didn't he?"

"I'd almost forgotten what kindness was like."

I nodded. "I know. But you're never going to be used like that again, and we're going to find a way to get all those memories out of you too."

"They get heavy," she said. "It's not too bad when I first wake up, I can push them to one side. But they get louder, and bigger, and heavier through the day, and then I don't know which are mine and which aren't anymore."

"I know." As I nodded, I could feel the scratch moving up and down. "I'm really sorry this has happened to you. To all of your people. It's so unfair."

"I guess you know what it's like too."

I shrugged. "To a much lesser degree. I hope you don't mind walking, by the way."

"Believe me, it's a million times preferable to being cooped up in that wagon all day."

I turned round and looked back at Tian. "Seriously, just come and walk with us."

He jogged to catch up. "If you insist."

I shook my head. "You're an idiot."

He grinned, and I couldn't help but smile back. And it was nice to have his company. He didn't take anything seriously, and it felt like I'd taken my whole life seriously. It was a nice change to be laughing and joking around.

Malia's shivers started to show as her arms began twitching.

"I'm sorry," she said. "I think I'll be gone again soon."

"You have nothing to apologise for," I said, taking hold of her hand.

"What's that?" said Tian, pointing at the road ahead.

"Maybe we should cut across country," I said quickly. "We probably shouldn't be out in the open, especially with Malia like this."

Tian cupped his hands over his eyes and squinted. "I think it's a person."

I looked. There was a hump at the side of the road; possibly a crouched figure. Another dark patch lay in the road. Was it someone lying down? I tugged Tian's sleeve.

"Let's get off the road."

"They might need help," said Malia.

"They might be waiting for someone to rob," I replied.

Tian frowned at me. "Is it your heritage that makes you so suspicious?"

"Is it yours that makes you so naive?"

"Let's just go and check on them. That looks like someone in the road. They might have been attacked themselves, or hit by a car."

"They might need help," Malia said again.

"Then I guess common sense loses this vote," I said with a sigh.

"You'd better get used to not being in control anymore," said Tian. "Looks like me and Malia are in tune with one another."

As we got closer, we could see that the figure crouched on the verge was a child, and the body in the road was some kind of animal. A dog perhaps. We could also see the boy's close cropped hair, his muddied clothing, the feather attached to his shirt. A rogue. I stopped, and grabbed both Tian and Malia by the arm.

"We need to get off the road. Now."

"It's just a child," said Tian. "What's he going to do?"

"It's probably a trap," I replied. "If you didn't know, people like him like to kill people like me."

"Not all rogues are bloodthirsty murderers. Some of them just want to live a quiet life on the fringes of society. Doesn't that sound a bit familiar?"

"And how do we find out what kind he is? Because I'm not too keen to test out your theory with me as bait, thank you very much."

Tian shook his head. "Always thinking of yourself."

"That's kind of the only reason I'm still alive. We're in rogue country now. There could be hundreds of them just waiting to ambush us once our guard is down."

"Listen to yourself. Rogues have bikes and guns. If they were wanting to kill you, they'd have done it already. Like flicking the cherry off the top of the pie." He demonstrated the motion in case I hadn't understood.

I looked up at the boy, and saw that Malia was already approaching him.

"Do you need help?" I heard her say.

"Looks like you've not got a choice anyway," said Tian.

As we approached the boy, I kept my eyes on the trees and rocks that surrounded us. The spaces between the cities were little more than wastelands, broken only by small, remote towns and farms. The rogues ruled these places; gangs that ignored the accepted norms and rules of society, and thought of themselves as beyond the reach of the law. Although their number was partly made up of traders who had abandoned colony life, they were well known for hunting down traders, sometimes wiping out whole colonies in one go. Just like Okaporo.

While Malia wrapped her arm around the boy's shoulders, Tian crouched down to the animal in the road. It was a dog, I could see that now, and it had clearly been hit by something. It was breathing fast, panting, and there was blood everywhere. It wasn't going to survive.

"We were just walking," the boy was saying. "I didn't even hear the car."

He was used to the noise of the rogue bikes. Despite being officially unavailable for several decades, the rogues got hold of petrol from somewhere to fuel their hybrid vehicles. But the auto-cars ran on either electric or hydrogen, and achieved high speeds with nothing more than a gentle hum. If you had your back to them, you didn't stand a chance of knowing they were there.

"He knows his way home," the boy continued between sobs. "I'm completely lost without him. He's my best friend."

My fingers twitched, my hand trying to lift itself to my heart. But I did genuinely feel sorrow for him. Even for him. Even a rogue.

Tian had moved from the dog, and was crouched next to the boy with Malia. He was shaking his head. "It's best to put him out of his misery. He's suffering, and you don't want him to hurt anymore, do you?"

It was a tough lesson to learn when you were so young, but this was a rogue child, he was probably used to death already.

The boy sniffed and nodded. He pulled a small gun from his bag, and I instinctively stepped back. "I don't even know how to use it," he said.

Everyone turned away as Tian put the bullet into the animal's skull. The sound of it seemed to ring on for ages, echoing around our heads and our hearts. I looked back at the boy. His lips were pressed tightly together, his red eyes roving around as he tried to be brave. My heart truly did ache for him. I knew what it was like to be suddenly alone in the world.

Malia helped the boy to his feet. "You can come with us now. We'll help you find your family."

"Hold on," I said, jogging over to them. "I don't think we can do that."

"Why not?" asked Malia.

I pulled Tian to one side. "What are we going to do? Walk up to the next rogue camp we find and ask them if they've lost a kid? I'm not suicidal."

"And what do you propose, we just leave him here to fend for himself?"

"He's armed, seeing as you handed him his gun back, so I think he'll be fine."

"He's just a child."

"Yes, that belongs to a band of rogues that will probably kill me on sight."

"You don't know that."

I threw my hands into the air. How did no one understand this? "Haven't we covered this already? What will it take for you to believe me? A bullet between my eyes? I didn't actually plan on dying today."

"They're hardly going to open fire when we're walking up to them with their lost child, are they?"

"And what if he turns on us?"

"He's just a child."

"With a gun."

Tian sighed and laid his hand on my shoulder. I shrugged it off.

"I'm not saying we have to walk into a rogue camp," he said, "but we can at least find him somewhere safe. We could leave him at a nearby farm or village, let them find out where he's come from. Just... we can't leave him sat at the side of the road staring at his dead dog."

I looked back at Malia. She was holding hands with the boy and watching me intently.

"Fine." I said.

"What's your name?" she asked the boy.

"Shrike."

I rolled my eyes. It was a joke among the rogues, to give their children bird names to mock us. Traders had used those terms for generations; the brood mothers, the rooks. Belittle people for long enough, and they become less than people to you. That's when you can fire a bullet into them and walk away without remorse.

"Fine, Shrike," I said. "Welcome to the gang. You better keep up."

And so we continued along the road. A trader, a carrier, a merchant, and now a rogue. Sworn enemies of one another. The whole time, I kept an eye on Shrike's bag where his gun jumped against his hip with every step.

As we walked, Malia chatted with Shrike. They played spotting games, and word games, and it seemed to keep Malia's shivers at bay. She'd never remained lucid this late in the day before. She laughed and sang and skipped, and you would never guess that she was a smudger.

Tian nudged me. "You see, it was a good idea after all."

"Well, I'm still withholding judgement on that

one."

"Can't you just admit when you're wrong?"

I looked at him. "If we survive this experience, it still doesn't prove me wrong. Rogues are dangerous. That's an undeniable truth."

"But this one is not."

"Yet."

Tian sighed. "Have you ever trusted anyone in your entire life?"

"Yes, thank you. I've trusted lots of people. And they all either died or let me down. Any other questions?"

"Yes. Who's that?"

Tian pointed at the road ahead of us where a small group of rogues were stood on the verge. I stopped.

Tian turned round and looked at Shrike. "Do you recognise any of them?" he asked.

Shrike squinted. "Yes!" Dropping Malia's hand, he pushed past Tian and ran towards the men. One of them stepped forward and grabbed Shrike up into his arms, spinning him around.

"I guess that's his family then," Tian said.

"Then our job is done," I replied. "Let's get out of here." I tugged at his sleeve.

"Hold on," he said.

One of the rogues was approaching us and my feet begged to step behind Tian. I silently cursed them and forced myself to stand strong. Head held high. I met that rogue eye to eye.

"You have nothing to fear from us," he said

straight to me. "You looked after Shrike when you could have abandoned him. I expect that was hard for you. I hope that I can, in some way, repay that favour. There's another band of rogues on your trail. They've been tracking you for some time. Some ridiculous notion about finishing what was started at Okaporo."

"Well, they're about ten years too late," I said as coldly as I could manage. I felt like I was melting inside, collapsing in on myself, but I willed my legs to stone. Out of the corner of my eye I saw Tian turn and look at me. He clearly knew the significance of that name. No doubt he'd want to ask me about it later.

The rogue shrugged. "Either way, your name is on their list. So just watch yourself. There's also news on the network of a trader and a merchant carrying something pretty valuable. I'm guessing that's the two of you. So you really need to stay alert. And, just a suggestion, but you might want to stay off the road too."

I nodded and looked at Tian.

"Look," the rogue continued, "we can watch you for a little while, but we certainly can't protect you the whole way, so you're on your own after that. This place is not safe for any of you."

"Thanks," said Tian. "We appreciate that. A lot."

"Thank you," I muttered.

"We're not all violent murderers, y'know."

I nodded.

"Stay safe." He nodded to us both, and then rejoined his friends. They all looked over at us for a second, before disappearing off into the trees.

21

SENETSU

Omori howled in my arms as cold rainwater ran down her face. We were all soaked through, freezing cold, and beyond desperate. My feet were sore in my sodden shoes and my arms ached from carrying Omori's weight. I had never felt so despairingly homesick.

Saji was negotiating at the door of yet another boarding house. I hitched Omori further up—her slick coat was so difficult to keep hold of—and buried my face into her dripping hair.

"I'm so sorry," I whispered. "I'm so sorry that this is our life."

My brain tried to think that maybe Mrs Rido was right, but I refused to let it. Omori was best with us, there was no question about it. I held her tighter, and looked up at Saji. He was waving his arms around, gesturing at me and Omori.

Finally he turned round and beckoned us to come. He stepped back and let me go inside first.

I stood in the hallway, Omori clinging to me, and dripped onto the linoleum floor. Omori was still wailing. She needed to be stripped, and changed into dry clothes, but even the spare clothes I'd taken from Mrs Rido were soaked through inside the rucksacks.

"I can't have that noise," the landlord said. The sympathy that had led him to invite us in had already waned. "If my other guests find out I've got traders here, they'll all leave. You'll have to go."

"I'll keep her quiet," I said quickly. "She just needs to get out of these wet clothes. I promise, we'll keep her quiet." I pulled Omori against me, rubbed her back, and silently begged her to calm down.

The landlord frowned, but relented with a nod. "Fine. But if I get a single complaint, you're back out, rain or no rain."

"We understand," said Saji. "Thank you. Thank you so much."

The landlord led us to a room which was actually more of a cupboard. It had one bed, slightly wider than a standard single, and a bedside table rammed against it. That was all there was room for. A tiny window near the ceiling dribbled water down the wall, and had left a permanent stain in its wake.

The landlord pointed at me, then at Saji, then back to me. "No noise. At all. And I don't want anyone seeing you going to the bathroom either."

I nodded. "We won't be any trouble." Omori clung to my wet coat, sobbing into its folds.

The landlord withdrew, and closed the door. I dropped Omori to the floor, and she collapsed to her knees.

"Stand up, darling."

"Where's Kioto?" she asked.

"Kioto isn't here."

"I want Kioto."

"Omori, stand up."

She didn't move. I pushed my hands under her arms and lifted her up to her feet, but she refused to stand, simply collapsing back down each time.

"Omori," I whispered sharply. "If you don't behave we're going to be kicked out of here back into the rain. Is that what you want? To sleep outside in the rain?"

Instead of scaring her into cooperating, my chastisement made her scream even louder. I held my hands up to Saji.

"I can't, I just can't," I said, my voice cracking with tears.

Saji scooped her up into his arms. "I'll put her in a hot bath. You get your wet clothes off and get some rest."

I nodded, sniffling like a child.

I woke to the sound of shouting, and it took me a moment to decipher what was happening. I opened my eyes and saw Saji wrestling Omori into the room.

She was shouting "Kioto! Kioto! Kioto!"

I jumped from the bed and clasped my hand over her mouth.

"Omori, you have to be quiet. If you shout they'll kick us out in the rain."

She quietened a little, but continued to call out her sister's name from behind my hand.

I pointed wildly at the rucksacks. "That bag, Saji. I picked up some medical supplies. See if there are any sleeping pills."

"We can't give a child sleeping pills."

"We'll just give her half of one."

He still didn't move.

"Come on, Saji, we can't have her like this all night."

He finally picked up the bag and began shaking its contents out onto the bed. Digging through them, he pulled out a bottle of tablets. He fumbled with the lid before getting it open. I took the half tablet he offered and pushed it into Omori's mouth.

"This will help you, darling. Swallow it down."

Saji passed me a bottle of water, and I handed it to Omori.

I looked up at him. I could see how much he hated to do this, and I hated it too. But I'd hated every single night watching her crying in her sleep, and holding her tightly, rocking her back and forth, while she'd sobbed for the home and the sister she'd lost. While we'd both sobbed.

I sat up on the bed with her, and pulled her in close. All of our clothes were wet, so I wrapped her in the thin duvet. I smoothed her hair while she cried into my chest, her hands gripped tightly around my neck.

"Just sleep, darling, get some sleep."

Omori shook her head and looked up at me. "When I sleep I see Kioto," she said. "And she's on fire."

"I think it's our only option right now," I said. I looked down at Omori, finally sleeping soundly.

Saji frowned and shook his head, but I could tell that he wasn't committed to his disagreement.

"To take all of her memories of her sister," he said. "That's extreme."

"It won't be forever. We'll give them back. I just... I can't bear to see her hurting anymore. She's emotionally and physically exhausted, and if she doesn't remember her sister, she'll be able to sleep. And she'll be able to build a future for herself. We can't spend our entire lives with our heads turned towards Okaporo. No matter how much of ourselves we left behind there. We have to concentrate on Omori now, and she needs to be able to move on."

"And we've got to remember that she can't be trained as a trader while she's missing memories. You know that. Even if one scrap of a memory is missing, she won't be able to train."

"Of course I realise that, but she's only four. That gives us two years to get settled into Kumonayo before she'd start her training anyway. When our lives are stable, when she's settled and feeling secure, then we'll give her those memories back."

"And what? Have her confused and scared? Have her not trust us because we've been lying to her?"

"We'll just have to figure it out when we get to it. I'm sorry that I don't have all the answers for you right now."

Saji sighed deeply. "I don't like it."

"Neither do I. But I also hate giving her tablets to get her to sleep."

Saji nodded. "I know. I guess..."

"It's not forever. Just until we get settled. I'll do it quickly while she's asleep. She won't even know it's happened. No one needs to know."

"No, we can't let anyone find out what we've done. You'd get hauled up in front of the brood mother just for performing an extraction on a child, but a child we've drugged into sleep? I dread to think what they'd do to you."

"So this is our secret," I said, rolling Omori onto her back. I didn't perform the Dedication. I didn't want the High present, I didn't want them to see what I was about to do. I lay one hand on Omori's warm stomach, and the other on her forehead.

She frowned and murmured as I pushed into her head. It was easy to find my way around her memories; there were so few of them compared to an adult. She'd already locked her memories of Kioto together; a dark, hard mass in her head like a tumour. It was impenetrable, vicious, malignant. I touched it, and pulled my hand from Omori's forehead as if I'd been burnt.

"What is it?" asked Saji.

"I can't do it. There's so much hurt there, so much pain. Saji, it would kill me to carry these memories alongside my own."

"Can't you lock them away? You take bad memories all the time, it shouldn't be any different."

I shook my head. "It's not the same as taking memories from a stranger. These are cohesive with my own memories. You can't just ignore them, or push them aside as an anomaly. I'd be playing them over and over, as well as my own. I can't do it, Saji."

He stepped forward and rubbed my shoulder. "It's ok. We'll get through this somehow. Kids are so resilient."

"You didn't see inside her head. Those memories, they're... She's too young to be carrying something like that. Who do we know in the Akimori colony?"

Saji thought for a moment. He grabbed his coat. "I know someone. I'll be back soon."

22

KIOTO

I looked up at the darkening sky. "We should look for somewhere to spend the night."

"You're right," Tian said. He pulled up a screen in front of him. "There's a town not far up—"

"No towns," I said. "No guest houses. For one, we're very unlikely to find one that would take either me or Malia. And for another thing, we really don't want to leave a trail. We don't want anyone seeing us, or being able to identify us. And the three of us together are pretty identifiable. If you want a nice comfy bed for the night, no one's stopping you."

"I'm not going to leave you two alone out here."

"Because we need you to protect us?"

He grinned. "Are you kidding? I was hoping

you'd protect me."

I punched him playfully.

"You see," he said. "You've got the killer instinct."

I laughed. "I can't believe I'm hanging out with a merchant."

He nudged me. "We're not all bad."

"Well, strictly speaking, you're a merchant of trader heritage. So I guess that makes it ok."

"As long as I live up to your high standards."

I eyed him. "Just about, I suppose."

"Look at that," he said, suddenly serious. I looked where he was pointing, and spotted the roof of a barn amongst some trees.

"Let's check it out," I said. I looked back at Malia who was still trailing behind us, muttering and twitching. I wished I could do something to help her. I just hoped someone at the Honporo colony could do something. I took hold of her hand and gave it a squeeze. She didn't seem to notice, but simply followed as we set off down the bank towards the barn.

I settled Malia down, and, exhausted, she quickly fell into a fitful sleep. It was tiring carrying other people's memories. They got heavy, particularly the bad ones.

I looked around for Tian. He was sitting on a crate flicking through a small screen in front of him. I wandered over.

"What are you looking at?"

"Just wondering if I can make it to the next town and back before it gets too dark. Get us some supplies for breakfast."

I nodded. "Sounds like a good idea. Reckon you can make it?"

"If I hurry." He stood up.

"Well, be careful. I don't want to find you lying face down somewhere with a broken neck."

"I'll have a scout around too, make sure there's no sign of any rogues following us. Except the ones that are keeping an eye on us, at least."

I huffed. "There's no one keeping an eye on us. If they are following us, they're probably just waiting for their chance to kill us first."

"What is your problem? If they'd wanted to kill us they have had plenty of chances."

I shrugged. "They're playing with us. Like cats with their prey."

Tian shook his head. "I better go if I'm going to be able to see to come back." He stood, and the screen moved with him.

"Can't you light your way with that?" I asked, gesturing at the illuminated screen hovering between us.

"It's not a torch." He patted me on the shoulder. "I'll be back soon."

I nodded. "We'll be here."

I watched him disappear into the dusk. I looked back over at Malia. She'd rolled over and her face was illuminated by our solar lanterns. She was frowning, and mumbling in her sleep. Maybe I'd ask Tian for another sleeping pill for her tonight. It was unfair to make her walk so far every day when she wasn't getting a proper rest at night.

I sat down and opened my bag, pulling out everything I needed for the Grace. I hadn't been strict enough about doing it every day, ending up rushing through it at dusk without the reverence it deserved. Of course, the ceremony had to be performed minus my pebble. The one remaining thing I had from my home.

It had been fully dark for some time when Tian finally reappeared, and I'd almost worn a trench into the floor pacing back and forth with worry.

"Where've you been?" I demanded.

"Shopping." He smiled at me, holding up two bulging bags.

"I thought you were just grabbing some breakfast for tomorrow."

"Just because we're sleeping in a barn, doesn't mean we can't eat like kings."

I shook my head. "Whatever."

Tian began unloading the bags. I looked at the array of what could only be described as snack foods. There was plenty of sugar, but not the slightest hint of a vegetable.

"What's all this?" I asked.

"I thought we'd have a movie night."

I gestured to the barn around us. "Movie night? Just one problem."

"Not a problem at all." Tian drew a screen between us and then threw the projection to the far wall of the barn, creating our own cinema. "Modern technology isn't all evil, y'know."

I took hold of one of his hands and inspected his thumb and forefinger. Tiny silver scars showed where the implants had been inserted. I pressed my thumb against them. They were tiny, but you could feel them. I shivered, and backed away.

"It's just creepy having something put in under your skin like that. Don't you ever worry that they might explode or something?"

Tian laughed. "It's never happened yet."

"But it could, couldn't it?"

He shrugged. "And I could get hit by a bus."

"Which are also meant to be perfectly safe and incapable of harming humans."

He grinned at me and dragged a couple of bales of hay over in front of the screen, gesturing for me to sit down. He sat next to me and drew out a smaller screen.

"What do you fancy?" he asked.

"You choose."

"I guess you're not really up to date with the latest releases, eh?"

I didn't answer.

Tian loaded a screen, and the opening credits started rolling. I'd seen movies before, watched TV, but it didn't fascinate me. I spent most of the time thinking of all the more useful things I could be doing. I looked around the barn. I guess I wouldn't have that problem today. Looking back up at the screen, I decided to try my best to enjoy it.

Tian pushed a packet of popcorn at me.

"It's popcorn," he said. "Try it."

"I'm not from some prehistoric age, I have had popcorn before."

"You don't seem like a sugar kind of person, that's all."

I grabbed a handful and stuffed it into my mouth, spilling half of it into my lap. I smiled broadly at Tian, my mouth full.

He burst out laughing, and I laughed too, spraying popcorn everywhere. He threw a handful of it at me, and I returned another.

"Stop, stop!" he spluttered, picking popcorn out of his hair. "You're not at all how I imagined you'd be."

"What do you mean?"

"You traders always seem so serious all the time. So… sanctimonious."

"It's an inherited facial expression, passed down through the generations. We have special classes on it and everything."

"That's why you all do it so well."

"Oh yes, our sanctimony is practised and perfected."

Tian looked at me for a moment. "Is it true what he said, that you're from Okaporo?"

I sighed. "I knew you'd ask. I'm surprised it took you so long. Yes, I'm from Okaporo."

"You must've been young when that happened. What is it, ten years ago now?"

"Eleven. I was eight years old."

"That must've been… I can't even imagine."

"I was away at the time. A whole bunch of us were on a trip to the Iwoyo colony with our rooks when it happened. We knew nothing about it at all until we returned late that evening. We thought we were going home, but we returned to a graveyard. The whole place had been burnt to the ground. Everyone and everything was destroyed. How can anyone imagine anything so devastating? It took me ages to even believe it had happened. I mean, tragedies are something that happen to other people, right?"

"What did you do?"

"Once the rooks had established no one was alive, we stayed long enough for them to bury the bodies, and then we set off for Kagosaka, our sister colony. Their brood mother became our brood mother."

"But you don't live there anymore?"

I shook my head. "It was meant to be our new home, but it never was. We were never accepted there, always thought of as outsiders. They used to make cuckoo noises at us. When you hear that every single day for eight years, it really starts to get to you. The brood mother did nothing, just ignored it. The rooks there? They joined in. The rooks from Okaporo weren't meant to be teaching anymore, but they used to teach us after dark, in secret, because we weren't getting the proper training. Kagosaka was never home."

"Do you think you'll ever belong to another colony?"

"I doubt it. Kagosaka kind of put me off ever trying anywhere else."

"I can understand that."

"After all, an important part of colony life is drawing from the wisdom of your ancestors. Mine are all still in Okaporo, buried under the scorched earth."

"Have you ever been back?"

I shook my head. "I've not even seen the sea. I've stayed as far away from the coast as possible. In Kagosaka, there was one place that when the wind blew in the right direction I could smell the salt, even taste it some days. I spent a lot of time sat there, pining for Okaporo. But when I left Kagosaka, I turned my back to it all. I had to make a clean break."

"And now we're headed for Honporo. Right on the ocean."

"Now we're headed for Honporo."

"What are you going to do after we've delivered this job?"

I looked over to where Malia still slept. "Get her emptied. I'm hoping someone in the colony there can help me. She's so full I can't do it without risking a rush."

"Why's she so important?"

I looked at him.

"I'm sorry," he said. "I know you don't want to say."

"Because she's got a memory from my little sister."

"You've got a sister?"

"I had a sister. She died in the massacre. At least,

I thought she did, along with my parents. But the glimpse of the memory I saw when Malia touched me suggests that they got away. They might even still be alive."

Tian stared at me, his mouth flapping open without any words to say.

"I know," I said, rescuing him. "It may well be that the last eleven years of my life have been a complete lie. What if more people escaped? What if we were sent away purposefully? If that's even halfway true it would mean that our brood mother, Narata, knew it was going to happen. And if that's true, then she had the chance to save everyone, but chose not to. Wow, it sounds even worse when I say it out loud. It's just..." I banged my head with the heel of my hand. "It's too much to be wondering about. I need to know for sure."

Tian looked over at Malia. "Now it makes sense. I didn't think you were that kind of person."

"What kind of person."

"The kind to kill another trader."

"What are you talking about?"

"Using the smudger as a weapon."

"Seriously, what are you talking about?"

Tian shrugged. "It's just something I've heard some of the merchants saying. That traders are buying up smudgers to use as weapons to kill other traders with."

I looked over at Malia. "Forcing a rush onto them."

"I don't know if it's true, but it's what some

people say."

I shook my head. "I can't believe that. Because, if you kill a trader with a rush, you're not just killing them, you're condemning their soul to eternal unrest. No trader would do that to one of their own."

"It's amazing what some people might do."

I shook my head again. "No. I can't believe that."

"I'm sure you're right."

I looked back at Malia. She was sleeping soundly at last, the shivers subsiding. Maybe if a brood mother could condemn most of her colony to death, then a trader really could be that depraved. I dragged my fingers back through my hair.

"This is just too many revelations in just a few days."

Tian took hold of my hand. "I'm sorry, I shouldn't have said anything."

"You didn't know that I was completely clueless."

"You're not completely clueless."

It certainly felt like it. People had been lying to me for years, and I couldn't stop running through my head everything anyone had said about Okaporo, my family, Narata, searching for evidence. Just the tiniest clue. It felt like my brain was on fire.

Tian shifted across closer to me. "Sorry. Tonight was meant to be fun."

I smiled at him. "Actually, it has been kind of fun. I can't even tell you the last time I talked to someone. I mean really talked to someone. And had them actually listen."

He squeezed my hand. "I'm glad I could be that

person for you."

"Who would've thought it would be a merchant?"

"Like you said; I'm only playing at being a merchant. I've got trader blood. You shouldn't be so quick to judge people."

"Keeping my distance from rogues and being suspicious of you guys is what's kept me alive. I can only judge people based on my own experience, and my experience of both rogues and merchants has been pretty crap. I do what I have to."

"I guess we all do."

He took hold of my other hand, and I felt the tingling run all the way up my arm. I closed my eyes as his lips pressed hard against mine.

23

SENETSU

I smoothed down Omori's hair. She had no idea what had just happened, and she wouldn't know any different when she woke either. Life would be normal, she just wouldn't know that she ever had a sister. We'd have to be careful not to mention Kioto's name in front of her.

"Thank you so much, Hama," Saji said, giving the Akimori trader a tight hug.

"I saw something when I was in her head." Hama looked from Saji to me, and back again. "She's... she's a vessel, isn't she?"

Saji nodded. "That's kind of how we ended up here."

"So you have to keep those memories safe for

us," I said. "We'll need them back for her to be trained. You know how important it is that she's trained up."

Hama nodded. "Sure, I mean the ability to be able to offload the memories we're carrying into a vessel is vital for the continuation of the colonies. It's fine for those merchants, offloading their extracted memories into their poor slaves, but we have to be more careful. We can only extract memories we know that we can sell, and sell quickly before we risk the shivers. To have a vessel means we can do so much more. We can actually compete with the merchants."

"And Omori isn't affected either," added Saji. "Those memories just pour straight out of her and into the ground."

"Is she staying here? In Akimori?" Hama asked.

"No, we're headed to Kumonayo. They're expecting us. Narata told us we'd be safe there."

Hama frowned. "Kumonayo? You're sure? I think she'd be far better protected in Akimori. Those hills around Kumonayo are crawling with rogues."

"But no one knows that we're here. And no one knows what Omori is. Except us, and now you."

"There's been a lot of whispers that a vessel was born, even all the way out here. And the Okaporo massacre just proves it, and proves where she was born."

"So everyone thinks she's dead."

"You know how whispers are. Even when there's irrefutable proof there are still people who will deny it. There's always some kind of conspiracy theory.

But with the lack of any identifiable bodies in Okaporo, the rumours are rife. Lots of people say the vessel made it out alive. And the hills there whisper more than anywhere else. You'll see what I mean when you get to Kumonayo."

"Narata said we'd be safe there. We trust her."

Hama shrugged. "I doubt you're safe anywhere. But Kumonayo, there's a lot of talk about the brood mother there, Tokai. There's talk that she's in with both the rogues and the merchants."

"But there's always talk like that."

"Well, I'm only saying what I've heard. And I've been there. There's a lot of money in that colony, and very little explanation as to where it comes from. Go if you must, but I wouldn't trust Tokai."

"Thank you for the warning. We'll watch ourselves." Saji glanced over at me, his face full of worry.

"Come to Akimori, we can look after you there. You'll be much safer."

"We need to stick to the original plan," I said. "There's been too much upheaval already."

Hama snatched up her ceremony items and stuffed them back into her bag. "Well, whatever. Just watch your backs, that's all I'm saying. You can't trust a Kumonayo trader, everyone knows that."

She slammed the door behind her as she left.

24

KIOTO

My eyes flicked open, and it took a moment for me to remember where I was. I lifted Tian's arm off me and sat up. What had woken me?

Then it came again.

"They're coming! They're coming to get you!"

I spun around. Malia was hopping from foot to foot, her face covered in scratches again.

"They're coming for you. For you. Now. There's no time. They're coming, they're coming!"

I shook Tian awake. He looked up at me with bleary eyes.

"What?" he mumbled.

"I think the rogues are on their way."

"What?" he said again.

I pointed at Malia.

"It's just the shivers. Some memory she's playing."

"But she never wakes up with the shivers."

He patted my hand. "She's going to get worse. You know that."

"I dunno, Tian. Something just tells me we need to go. And I always trust my gut."

I started packing everything away into my bag.

"Does this mean we don't get breakfast?" Tian asked, packing his own things.

"Not right now, no."

I grabbed Malia and dragged her from the barn. I quickly scanned the landscape around us, and headed for the highest spot I could see. Tian trailed behind, picking up things he dropped along the way while simultaneously pulling on his coat. He clearly wasn't used to such a rushed exit. I, however, was quite used to them.

I pushed Malia up ahead of me, and she was still shouting "They're coming for you! They're coming! Go now! Go now! Go!"

"Can't you get her to be quiet?" Tian panted behind me.

"What do you want me to do, gag her?"

"I don't know, just something. Because if your gut is right, she's going to lead those rogues right to us."

"I thought rogues were nice. I thought I just judged them too quickly."

"When they're ones that we know are after us

because they know we're carrying something valuable, with rogues like that, I'm not willing to find out whether they're nice or not. I'm going to make a snap judgement on that."

At the top of the hill, I huddled behind an outcrop of rocks, pulling Malia down to the ground with me. I took hold of her face in my hands, and turned her towards me.

"It's ok, we've got away, we're safe now. But you need to be quiet. Can you do that?"

"They're coming," she whispered. "They're coming."

"I know they are, but just keep quiet."

I turned to Tian. "Do you hear that?" I whispered.

He listened. "Engines," he confirmed.

"She was right."

"As was your gut."

From where we were, we watched five bikes run through the valley below, passing right next to the barn we'd been sleeping in. They stopped, and one of them looked inside. And then they circled back the way they'd come.

"That's how close it was," I said.

I reached out and took hold of Malia's hand. She was shaking her head violently, and the motion was passing down through her whole body.

"She's not good," I said. "We really need to get to Honporo."

Tian pulled up a screen. "And there aren't any more colonies along the way to stop at for help."

"I know. I'm going to have to do it myself. Just try

to take some of the memories."

"You can't, you know what will happen."

I nodded. "A rush. It's a risk, but it's not a certainty. Maybe if I'm just really careful."

"Her head is like an overfilled balloon. You don't take a pin and start prodding at it just to let a bit of the air out, do you?"

"I have to do something."

"We'll just have to get Honporo quicker."

"Yeah sure, I'll just get my auto-car out of my bag, shall I?"

Tian thought for a moment. "We'll walk to the town and try to get a bus."

"One problem." I pushed back my hair and pointed at my scars. "No bus will take me. And they're unlikely to take Malia either."

"Can't you wear a hat, or a hood, or something to cover them?"

I stood up and turned around. "It's not just my scars that mark me out as a trader. My clothes, my hair, the colour of my skin. They don't need to see the scars to reject me. What if you take Malia. If you give her a sleeping pill she'll keep quiet. Take her to the colony."

"And they'll help me will they? A merchant turning up with a topped out smudger asking for help?"

I grunted. "No. Of course they won't."

"Then we just need to cover as much ground as we can as quickly as we can." He stood up and hitched his bag onto his shoulders. "Let's get going."

25

KIOTO

We walked almost solidly until dusk, making only quick stops to eat.

"Why didn't you buy proper supplies?" I snapped at Tian. "I am so sick of popcorn."

"Next time you can write me a shopping list. I wasn't exactly planning on some kind of extreme survivalist experience."

"Out here you should be prepared for anything."

"This isn't exactly normal for me."

"I'm so sorry that I can't offer you a golden palace out in the middle of sodding nowhere, your highness." I was tired, and fed up, and I could hear myself being completely unreasonable, but I couldn't stop. And it was easy to take it out on Tian. "We need to find somewhere for the night. I need sleep, and Malia definitely does."

Her shivers had got significantly worse, and even walking had become difficult against the constant flurry of ticks. I didn't know how much longer she could survive them, but she seemed to be strong willed and determined. That would certainly help her.

Scanning the horizon, there was no sign of any barns. The land here was dry, flat, and rocky. There were no farms because nothing could grow out here. You couldn't even graze animals.

"I think our only hope is to look for some kind of cave," Tian said. His voice had lost its usual edge of humour.

"You're probably right."

We trailed around the area for some time, doubling back on ourselves, walking in circles, before we finally found a formation of rocks that offered up a shallow cave. We were too exhausted to look for anywhere better, and the sun had already disappeared below the flat horizon.

I ducked inside the cave and unclipped my bed roll from my bag. I laid it out and guided Malia to it. She sat, but my efforts to encourage her to lie down were met with desperate scrabbling and wide, panicked eyes.

"No, no!" Malia screamed, her voice echoing around the rocks. "You'll kill her! She can't breathe!"

"You have to quieten her," Tian hissed, searching through his bag. "I'll get the sleeping pills."

"Ssshhh, ssshhh." I tried to soothe her. I cuddled her close, stroked her hair, but everything I did seemed to intensify her shivers even more. She writhed in my arms, screaming and howling. I let go of her and she crawled onto my bed roll, her shouts subsiding into whimpers and groans.

I looked at Tian and we sat in silence, listening. I'd never heard such silence before. There were no plants moving in the wind, no scratching of nocturnal animals, no chirping of crickets, or calling of birds settling into their roosts for the night. There was nothing but our breathing. And then we both heard it. The sound of engines.

"We need to go," I whispered.

"No," replied Tian. "You need to go. You and Malia. I'll lead them off, give you a head start."

"What are you on about? We both need to go."

"The rogues don't want me."

"They want what's in your head."

Tian winked. "Only if it is in my head."

"What?"

"Take my half of the scratch. Take it to the delivery and get my share of the money. Then get Malia the help that you need."

"And what about you?"

"I'm just a guy out in the wilderness. Nothing even marks me out as a merchant. They have absolutely no need for me. Once they find nothing of worth in my head, they'll let me go. What reason do they have to keep me?"

"That's a risky assumption."

"What other choice do we have? If we all run, they will catch us. We can't outrun their bikes on foot. But I lead them away, you can get somewhere safe."

I reached out and grabbed hold of his hand. "And we'll never see each other again."

He squeezed my hand in reply. "I'll find you. Come on, we're out of time. Take the scratch."

I grabbed my bag and dug through it, pulling out my bowl, my rabbit pelt—

"What are you doing? There's no time for messing about, just do it." He pushed the pelt and bowl back into my bag.

He lay down and I placed one hand on his forehead, and the other on his stomach. My hands were sweaty, my heart hammered, and I could barely focus. I pushed into his head, and I felt the sharp edges of the scratch as he pushed it forward. I took hold of it and withdrew, pulling it out into my own head.

"Now go," he whispered.

"Please don't die," I whispered back. I grabbed Malia's hand and pulled her to standing. I snatched up my bed roll and we set off at a run, the bed roll trailing behind us like a banner. My head was full of my own heartbeat, the heavy sound of my breathing. My legs carried me forward without me even having to think about them.

Because all I could think was that that might have been the last time I ever saw Tian, and that the last stupid words I said were 'please don't die'.

26

SENETSU

When we walked in through the gates of the Kumonayo colony, the city's high rises stretching up behind it, the first few people to see us started running, ahead of us, aiming to be the first to tell people that we had arrived. Keen to be the herald.

Within minutes, the brood mother, Tokai, approached us, surrounded by an eager crowd. Without a word, she embraced us each in turn, covering us in kisses. She took hold of Omori's head, pulling her hair back from her face, inspecting her.

She straightened up, and stepped back. Then she placed her hand on her heart and bowed her head. Everyone else around them imitated the motion. It was grotesque. A full cast performance of heartache, a recital of affinity. I almost expected them to take a bow afterwards and wait for our applause.

Omori looked up at me with questions in her eyes.

"Welcome to Kumonayo," Tokai said. "We're so glad to have you here, and thankful that you have arrived safely with us. Come, come, let's get you something to eat."

I glanced at Saji. "Actually, we're more tired than hungry. If you don't mind."

"Of course, of course. We already have a house set aside for you. It''s small, but it's private. Set aside from the others. I thought you might find it easier to settle if you weren't in the centre of everything."

"That's very thoughtful," Saji said. "Thank you."

"Want to go and see our new home?" I asked Omori, squeezing her hand.

She grinned and nodded. "Do I get my own bedroom?"

"Let's go and see shall we?"

In Okaporo, Omori and Kioto had had separate rooms, but they'd asked Saji to take down the wall between them. They had separate beds, but always chose to sleep cuddled together in one.

It hurt that she was so keen for a space by herself, and it hurt even more that we had done that to her. That her sister could be so easily erased and replaced by a desire to be alone. I'd almost expected, or hoped at least, that Omori would have an inexplicable feeling that something was missing, that she'd lost one half of herself. But she appeared to be relishing the detachment. Excited by the freedom. I had to remind myself that it wasn't conscious, or intentional. As far as she knew, she was an only child, and she always had been.

The houses in Kumonayo were nothing like the makeshift, scavenged dwellings of Okaporo. They were professionally built, fully hooked up to electricity, water, sewage. Several of them reflected the sky in solar panels, and at one edge of the colony, a pair of turbines rotated lazily.

Our new house was a small, two bedroom property, laid out over a single storey. It offered a double bedroom for Saji and myself, and a generous single room for Omori. It had a separate living room, and a kitchen large enough to include a dining area. It was fully furnished, and ready for us to move in.

"This is more than generous," I said to Tokai.

"You're special guests. Narata was a dear friend of mine, and this is my last promise to her. You'll be safe here in Kumonayo, I promise you that."

I looked up at Saji. It was clear that he'd also noticed the use of Narata's name in the past tense. Our last hopes faded; no one survived the massacre in Okaporo.

Tokai backed up towards the door. "I'll leave you to get some rest and settle in. The kitchen's fully stocked for you, so you don't need to worry about that. I'll drop by late morning tomorrow and see if there's anything you need. Get some rest for now, though."

"Thank you," Saji said again.

"Can I see my bedroom?" Omori asked, dancing from foot to foot.

"Of course you can. I'll unpack your things and you can decide exactly where you want everything to be."

We found everyone in Kumonayo to be more than helpful, and warmhearted, and kind. But I couldn't shake the feeling that, like the hands on heart gesture, it was nothing more than a performance. And I couldn't forget what Hama had said after Omori's memory extraction; that you couldn't trust a Kumonayo trader. I felt it too, but was it just because I was looking for it?

I sat outside our house in the early morning sunshine, watching the colony waking up and starting its day. Several people looked over and waved, but they didn't approach. We were being kept at arm's length. Or maybe we were keeping ourselves there.

I looked up as Saji placed a hand on my shoulder and handed me a steaming mug of coffee. I wrapped my hands around it gratefully.

"Thank you," I said.

He sat on the bench next to me. "You feel it too, huh?"

"Feel what?"

"That something's not quite right here. It's all just a little off. People are too nice and too generous."

"I just can't forget what Hama said about this place," I said.

"Me neither. She was certainly right about the

money being here, although I haven't seen any merchants coming in or out."

"Maybe that's why we've been put here, at the far end of the colony."

Saji shrugged. "Perhaps."

"I'm glad it's not just me being paranoid."

"To be fair, it might just be both of us being paranoid."

I took a sip of my coffee. "Have you heard the whispers?" I asked.

Saji nodded. "I thought it was just the wind at first, tried to convince myself of that. But I swear I hear Kioto's name on it sometimes."

I shivered. "Me too. There's just something not right here. I don't trust this place."

"Tokai mentioned to me yesterday that she's already chosen a rook for Omori."

"What? She's only four."

"Tokai said it was important to be prepared. That training Omori as a vessel needed a very special rook. I haven't met her yet, but Tokai said she'll come and see us soon to start discussing Omori's education."

"They're rushing things." I shifted round to face him. "We don't tell anyone that she's had an extraction, ok? Those memories are safe, we know that. Let's keep them out of her for now. Protect her from whatever Tokai's planning. If she can't be trained, then she's no use to them. Agreed?"

"Agreed."

"And I'll head out to the exchange today, start

looking for some jobs. We need to make sure we've got some money in our accounts just in case we need to get out of here in a hurry."

"That's a good idea."

I shook my head. "We've only just arrived, and we're already planning on running away."

Saji took hold of my hand.

"Is anywhere safe for us?" I asked him. He didn't answer.

27

KIOTO

The rain hammered into the ground, turning it into a quagmire. We huddled under a tree, but it offered scant protection from the weather. Huge drips of water ran down our backs, and a cold wind blew through our wet clothes, chilling them against our skin.

I looked at Malia. She was coping well; her survival instinct overriding the shivers, and making her quite lucid and rational.

"We need to find some proper shelter," she said, the cold turning her sentence into a stammer.

"You're right. I think there's another town up ahead, I think I saw some lights. But there's no guarantee we'll find anywhere to stay. These remote towns are even more backward than the cities in their attitudes towards traders, plus we're in rogue country, we can't trust anyone, especially someone who shows us any kindness."

"Maybe we could find an outbuilding."

"There's a chance. Do you want to risk it?"

Malia nodded. "If we stay here much longer we're likely to freeze to death anyway. I don't think our situation can really get much worse."

"You're right. Let's make a break for it."

The rain meant that no one in the town was out. Doors were bolted, curtains were drawn, shutters closed. The roar of water also covered any sound we made. We searched the area until we found a shed at the end of a large garden. It was far enough from the house that we wouldn't be seen. There was some goats already resident, but I'd shared beds with far worse in the past.

The shed boasted a number of pens, and we found an empty one to bed down in.

Malia began to remove her wet clothes.

"Keep them on," I said. They'll dry on you as you sleep, but if you take them off, they'll still be wet in the morning." I pulled my thick blankets from my bag and laid them on the ground. They were wet through. Looking around, I spotted a pile of goat blankets. They stank, and were covered in stuff that I didn't want to ponder on for too long, but they were dry. I laid them out on top of our wet blankets and gestured for Malia to lie down.

"This will dry the blankets out too. Cover yourself over with some straw. It'll be scratchy, but it will keep you warm."

"You're lucky you're so practical."

"Years of experience. And not good experiences, either."

"My life hasn't exactly been luxury."

I sat down next to her, and covered my lap with straw. "How long have you been a carrier?" I asked. "You don't have to tell me, if you don't want to."

"I was born into it. Both my parents are slaves. Or were. I don't even know if they're still alive or not. Carriers don't really have a very long life expectancy."

"I guess not. Do you know where your family is from, originally?"

"My parents were both born in Kolpanga, but my ancestors, as far as I know, were from Kumini. Or, Kanaoka as it's called now. I don't know for certain, though."

"Have you ever been there?"

"Once or twice, perhaps. When you're travelling around in the back of a merchant's wagon, everywhere kind of looks the same after a while."

My phone beeped and I pulled it from my pocket. I wiped the sheen of rainwater from the screen.

"It's Tian," I said, sitting upright.

"He made it?"

"He's asking if we're alive." I quickly sent a reply. We sat in silence waiting for him to respond. The minutes ticked by.

"Do you think it's really him?" Malia whispered.

I hadn't even thought about it. "If he asks where we are, I won't say." I smiled at her. "I guess we've both been conditioned not to trust anyone."

My phone beeped and we both jumped. "He just says to play the scratch, and to do what my heart tells me to." I looked at Malia. "What do you think that means?"

Malia shrugged. "I guess it will make sense if you play the memory."

"I guess." I lay down next to Malia and took a deep breath. She turned onto her side, putting her back towards me. It was all the privacy she could offer. I felt nervous; Tian's message suggested that this might change my plans to go to Honporo, my plans to deliver the memory. Which meant this memory would be somehow important to me.

I closed my eyes and pulled the scratch forward, putting the two pieces together. I'd never quite got used to the odd feeling of playing someone else's memory. It was the same process as remembering one of your own, but it was unfamiliar. It was disorienting, confusing. Like someone telling you something about yourself that you didn't know. That's why I usually left them alone.

Scratches never played properly anyway; they were incomplete memories. Sometimes they were accidentally extracted along with another, related memory. More often, though, they had been ripped; stolen from someone's head without their permission. Such memories, known as reds, were illegal, and the punishments were severe. Just imagine the harm that could be done if traders and merchants could go around stealing memories whenever they chose to.

The playback was jumpy. The sound wasn't always clear, and the picture was fuzzy. But Tian thought that this was important.

I could see the outline of two people in front of me, but they were just shadows. The view turned, and I was looking at a smaller, crouched figure, a child perhaps. And then the sound came, out of sync with the picture.

"You're right. I have a very grave matter to discuss. An important mission."

The playback crackled.

"The rogues know that the vessel is here. And they're coming for it."

"When?"

"Now."

"Now?"

"In a matter of minutes, I'd guess."

"How did they find out?"

"I don't know."

The playback cut and restarted as I found the tear between the two halves. Tian's part was more degraded.

"I trust in it completely. So I need you both to leave, straight away—Kumonayo."

"Kumonayo? That's the other side of the country. It's not even a sister colony."

"It's the only place that's safe for you right now."

The picture darkened, and the sound came and

went. I could barely catch any of the words at all. In the static, I thought I heard my name, but I dismissed it. People automatically looked for familiar sounds in white noise.

"—no time."

"Leaving her to—death?"

"—safely away—Okaporo will live on."

"—need to go."

"—asking us to—between our children."

"None of us have a choice anymore."

"What about the rest of you?"

"There's just no time—we must protect her at all costs. All costs."

As the view swung round back to the crouched figure, it flickered into clarity, showing me the perfect view of my little sister's face.

28

KIOTO

I lay in the darkness and looked up at the wooden ceiling above me. Outside, the rain continued relentlessly.

We were almost halfway to Honporo and almost two weeks away from Kumonayo. If we continued to Honporo to deliver the job, collect the money, find some help for Malia, it turned a two week journey to Kumonayo into almost four. But would Malia survive a two week journey?

I concentrated on the numbers, the distances, the times, because thinking about the memory, and the revelations it had exposed was more than I could cope with.

I needed to get those memories out of Malia, I

needed the full story. I couldn't let those memories die with her. But the scratch I carried, if that got into the hands of rogues, then my sister—who I'd thought was dead for the past eleven years—this scratch would be her death warrant.

This was too big. Too important. And every option I had was too risky. I needed to make a decision quickly, and stick to it, no matter the consequences.

In my heart, I knew I'd already made the choice. Tian was right: I had to follow it. We had to head for Kumonayo.

We woke to more dark skies, but the torrential downpour had relented to a misty drizzle. Malia washed quickly under a tap of cold water, while I plotted our route. She had accepted the change of direction without question.

I closed my eyes and quickly asked the High for a miracle. They weren't famed for being generous with miracles, but there were a few traditional stories of them being performed. Maybe they'd be feeling generous today.

I packed up our stuff, and, hoods up, we headed out into the morning.

This town was a different place in daylight. Despite its modest size, the town was crammed with people. A large market had sprung up in the centre, and people were pressed in around the stalls, the air above them filled with stallholders calling out their prices, morning gossip, and the smells of bread, cakes, fish, roasting meat, blacksmiths' furnaces, freshly sawn wood still hot from the blade.

We made our way through the crowd, and I heard the usual words muttered under people's breath as we passed by them.

"Earwigs."

"Reds."

"Rippers."

"Colony scum."

It should have been nothing more than white noise to me now. Malia bowed her head and followed closely behind, her hand gripping mine tightly.

As we broke free of the market crowd, I stopped and looked around. Three narrow streets led away in front of us. At the entrance to one, a group of girls were playing a skipping game, their legs moving quickly across two ropes.

One of the girls looked up at me and grinned. I didn't return the smile. Hers was neither friendly nor genuine. And then she began to sing.

"Cross your eye,

I hope you die,

And pray you never trip.

Once you're down,

And sleeping sound,

They'll rip, rip, rip!"

It was a crude, tuneless chant, but it had the desired effect. I backed away, and Malia's hand tensed in mine.

A few of the doors in the street opened, and women stepped out, staring up at us. Some even collected their husbands who appeared at the doorways brandishing improvised weapons: sticks, brooms, axes. The girls began to sing again.

"Cross eyes, reds, and rippers,

They'll leave you with the shivers,

If they get inside your head,

You'll wish that you were dead.

Give them a smudge to go,

Then kill them in the throw."

I stepped back again, and nudged Malia with my hip. "We need to get out of here," I said to her.

We moved back into the relative safety of the market. At least we could disappear a little in here. I pulled my hood further up over my hair, and we pushed our way back through.

An arm landed on mine. "You probably want to get out of here," its owner said.

"I'm trying," I muttered, looking up into the face of a merchant. Behind him, the eyes of his carriers peered out of his wagon, accompanied by fingers with their nails chewed back.

"This isn't the friendliest of towns for my kind, but you? You're brave for coming within a mile of this place."

"I'm quickly realising that."

"Where are you headed?"

For a moment, I considered lying, or telling him where to stick his curiosity. But I wondered if this might just be the miracle I'd asked for.

"Kumonayo. You're not headed that way, are you?"

The merchant's eyebrows jumped up his forehead before digging back into a frown. "Yes, with a few stops along the way."

"Can we ride with you?"

"I'm not a passenger service."

"I can pay."

He opened his mouth, but a thought seemed to stop whatever he had been about to say. His eyes flicked from side to side as he worked the thought through his head.

"With what?" he asked hesitantly.

"I have credit, or I have a memory I can trade."

"What kind of memory?"

"A young woman being attacked."

"What would I do with that?"

I cocked my head. He wasn't fooling me. "You know perfectly well that there's a thriving market for that. Men who like to pretend they did it. It's worth 200 at least." It was easily worth more than that, but I wanted him to think he was getting the better end of the deal.

"I'll give you 100 for the memory, and I'll take 100 in credit."

"Done," I said, without hesitation.

"And you both ride in the back with the carriers. I have no interest in making small talk with a trader the whole way."

"Not a problem," I replied. The feeling was entirely mutual.

He placed his hand onto my forehead, and I felt him begin to probe. I pushed the memory forward and he took hold of it. His presence scratched around on its way back out; he was either very poorly trained, or he was trying to have a nose around. But protecting my privacy was one of the first basics my rook taught me. It was preschool level. This merchant was an idiot. I was thankful I'd be in the back of his wagon and we could pass on that small talk.

29

KIOTO

Five days later, the wagon drove us into Kumonayo colony. As I climbed out of the vehicle, I looked around. This was not like any colony I'd ever seen before. It looked more like the city's suburbs.

I turned to thank the trader, and to suggest his swift departure, but he was already deep in conversation with a woman I guessed to be the colony's brood mother. Any other colony I'd known, he'd have been chased out as soon as he arrived. Something wasn't right here.

I touched Malia's arm. "Stay close," I whispered.

I wasn't even sure that she heard me; it was late afternoon, and she was muttering and twitching.

The brood mother finally turned to me.

"Welcome to Kumonayo," she said. "I'm afraid I have urgent business to attend to, but if you go into the community hut, you'll find all the hospitality you need."

I nodded my thanks and turned in the direction she'd pointed. Far from being a hut, the community building was a vast hall, the inside of which was laid out with tables and benches, with a long serving counter at one end. There were small gatherings of traders; eating, talking, playing games. At one table, a class of girls were gathered around their rook for a lesson.

"They're coming for you!" shouted Malia.

I rubbed her arm. "It's alright, we're safe now," I said soothingly.

Her outburst had attracted attention, and most of the eyes in the room were now focussed on us. But that turning of heads was quickly followed by a collective shrug of shoulders, and the heads turned back to what they were doing. The curiosity dissipated. I was expecting questions, whispers, assumptions, judgement, maybe even fear. But nothing came.

I crossed to the service counter and dished up two meals from under the hot lights.

Malia hardly ate anything. In fact, she could barely even hold her fork. Her twitching became progressively worse until she could barely sit on the bench. Her vocal ticks became louder and more desperate. She repeatedly cried out for me to help her, but I couldn't tell if that was one of her carried memories surfacing, or if it was a moment of Malia breaking through them. Either way, I didn't know what I could do.

I looked up as the brood mother sat down next to me. She nodded at Malia.

"She's pretty bad, isn't she?"

"Can you help her?" I asked.

The brood mother shrugged. "Maybe. I'm Tokai. What's your name?"

"Kioto. And this is Malia."

I watched the shocked look of recognition pass over her face with satisfaction.

"So my parents were here," I said.

"Yes." She looked hard at me. "I see it now. You look a lot like your mother."

"Do I? I haven't seen her since I was eight."

"No, of course not." Her hand raised to her heart for a moment. The ghost of a gesture.

"I don't suppose they're still here? And my sister?"

Tokai looked at the table, and then focussed on some point behind my head. "Your parents are, in a way. But I'm afraid they've passed on."

"Both of them?"

"I'm afraid so."

I nodded, feeling nothing. Until a week ago I'd thought they'd been dead for eleven years. I'd already done my mourning for them.

"What about my sister?"

"She's moved on." Tokai shifted in her seat. "Would you like to visit your parents' graves? Say goodbye?"

"I would."

"I'll ask someone to get Malia settled for a rest. See if they can calm her down a little. We'll have a peek inside her head and see if there's anything we can do to ease her suffering."

"Thank you. I'd been giving her sleeping tablets, but I don't have any left."

Tokai gestured to two traders who hurried over. "We'll find something to settle her," Tokai said to me. She turned to the traders and spoke to them quietly.

I touched Malia's arm. "I'll be back soon. You'll be looked after here. Hopefully they'll be able to help you."

Her eyes were glazed and looking at something no one else could see. I didn't know if she'd heard me.

Tokai turned back to me. "Come on."

I followed her away from the colony and towards the long grasses of the hills that surrounded Kumonayo. We passed by the ancestral graves, marked by rings and spirals of stones, flags, banners, ribbons, jewellery, statuettes. On the slopes of a hill, Tokai stopped. She gestured towards the ground. "Here."

I looked around me. "Here? Unmarked?"

"It's what Saji—your father—requested."

"They're not with the ancestors?"

"He thought this was more appropriate. I'm afraid your parents did little to integrate themselves while they were here. They kept themselves to themselves, remained as outsiders. When Senetsu passed on, Saji requested an unmarked grave for her away from the other burials. A few days after her death, he made me promise that, when his time came, he would be buried next to her. I should have watched him more closely, I should have understood what him asking that meant. And I blame myself. Less than a week after your mother's death, he took his own life."

"How do you know they're here?" I asked. "Exactly here. What makes you so sure that they're not there?" I pointed to my left. "Or there?" I pointed to my right. "Or on a different hill entirely?"

Tokai placed her hand on my shoulder. "Because these things are important. They haven't been forgotten, and they're visited regularly. No one leaves tokens here because it's what Saji asked. But they're not simply being left here to rot. I promise."

"And what about Omori? You said she'd moved on. Where did she go?"

"It was considered that her education would be better handled elsewhere. Because...." She drifted off.

"It's fine, I know what she is."

Tokai nodded. "Then I can speak honestly. Your parents, for their own reasons that I will never truly understand, had some of Omori's memories extracted before they arrived here. It was almost a Purification. They took almost everything away. As you know, that made it impossible to train her as a trader, let alone a vessel. However, that fact doesn't stop the rogues from hunting her. We thought it best if she was hidden elsewhere, outside of the colony, until we could restore her missing memories."

"Who has them?"

Tokai looked down at the ground. "That is a secret that died with them, I'm afraid."

"Did they say why they did it?"

"Not really. Just mumblings about it being 'necessary' or 'the best thing for everyone'. It was almost as if they didn't want Omori to be trained up."

"Why wouldn't they want that?"

Tokai didn't respond, and simply left the question hanging on the wind. "Let's go and see how your smudger's doing, shall we?"

She turned and marched back towards the colony. I crouched down and placed both hands on the damp ground.

"I'll find her," I whispered. "I promise."

30

KIOTO

"Where are you going to go?" asked Tokai, watching me pack my things into my bag.

I shrugged. "Not sure yet. Maybe head towards the coast. I've not seen the sea since... Well, it would be nice to connect with my ancestors."

"Roots are important. But you have your parents here. Why don't you stay for a while? The sun's barely even risen. I'm sure Malia would appreciate some more rest."

Malia smiled. "I've kind of got used to heading out at the crack of dawn with this one."

"I'm sorry that we couldn't help you. You're so topped out. Any attempt at an extraction would almost certainly result in a rush. It's just far too risky.

But I'm sure that comes as no surprise to you, does it?"

"Sadly not," I replied.

Malia nodded. "Kioto already tried, but she barely had to touch me to know it was too dangerous."

"Stay for a little while," Tokai urged again. "I have a lot of contacts. If there's anyone who can help, I'm sure to be able to find them."

"Thanks, but I've got a friend I need to find. We'll pop by again before leaving Kumonayo."

"You're staying in the city?"

"For a few days. Before I decide what to do next."

Tokai stepped closer to me. "You shouldn't look for Omori, if that's what you're thinking of doing."

"Not to be rude, but it really has nothing to do with you anymore."

Tokai grabbed hold of my wrist. "You have no idea what the vessel really is, what it can do. Besides, Omori has no memories left of you. She doesn't know that she ever had a sister. Leave her alone."

"It has nothing to do with you," I repeated.

"If you go storming into her world, telling her things she doesn't understand, you'll ruin everything for her. She needs stability, not confusion. The vessel is far more powerful than you imagine. Dangerous. Stay away from her."

I took hold of Malia's hand. "I have a band of rogues on my tail. You better pray to the High that they don't track me here. You wouldn't want another massacre like Okaporo."

My legs were shaking as I walked out of the colony, and I forced myself not to look back.

"At least now you know your sister's still in Kumonayo," Malia whispered.

I nodded. "I do. And her insistence that I stay away from Omori only makes me want to find her more. Besides, we have something no one else does. We have all her memories. She's the only person that can help you, and you're the only person who can help her. And we're the only ones that know that."

I heard footsteps behind us, and I quickened my pace. But the footsteps were running, and quickly caught up with us.

"Wait," the young trader gasped, trying to catch her breath. "Wait. It's not fair that Omori doesn't know who or what she is. It's not fair that she's being used the way that she is. I want to help you."

She passed me a scrap of paper.

"That's the name of the family she's with. That's all I know, I don't know where they live, but it won't be difficult to find them."

"Why do you want to help me?" I asked.

"I was friends with your sister. One day she made me promise that, if I ever met you, I'd do what I could to help. She never mentioned you again after that, and she'd never spoken of you before. I don't know what was special about that day."

"So she does know about me?"

"There are secrets in the colony, and in the hills, and the long grasses. They whisper them, but you have to listen closely. I hope you find the truth." She smiled, nodded, and ran back the way she'd come.

I looked at Malia and then down at the paper in my hand. I folded it into my pocket. "Let's find my sister," I said.

PART TWO

31

KIOTO

"This is utterly pointless," I muttered. I tugged my hood further forward, but the rain was coming in at us sideways, so it offered scant protection. "We've been standing out here for three days now, and we haven't seen any evidence of her being here at all. How do we know this is even right?" I pulled the slip of paper from my pocket, the fold in it so worn that it had almost become a hole.

Malia twitched her head "We could even be on the wrong side of the building."

I hadn't even thought of that. Three days, and it hadn't entered my head that we might just be standing in the wrong place.

"Do you suppose there might be another

entrance?"

"There's only one way to find out." She looked up at the block. "Either way, there's a lot of windows that she could be behind."

"Or none of them at all. Maybe we should make more enquiries."

"We don't want to draw too much attention to ourselves." Malia turned around and tugged my sleeve. She gestured with her head; just the tiniest of movements.

I peered out from behind the drips that clung to the edge of my hood. A warden of the peace was walking up the other side of the road. Wardens were at the bottom of the police hierarchy, little more than clerks, but if there was a job no one else wanted to go out for, like if it was pouring with rain and didn't promise an adrenaline-fuelled manhunt, they were called upon. Armed up with a stun gun and an over-inflated sense of importance. If there was any rank of the police likely to completely overreact and go in heavy-handed, it was a warden.

I turned as well, and feigned serious interest in the menu displayed in the window of the café we were now facing.

I heard footsteps approaching, a slight squelch under one shoe, and I tugged Malia's sleeve.

"Let's go," I hissed. Heads down against the weather, we started to walk.

The footsteps quickened behind us. An auto-car hummed past, hit a puddle, and the warden cursed. At least I had that. His feet were soaked.

"Ladies," his voice finally boomed.

I slowed, but we didn't stop.

"Ladies," he repeated. His hand grabbed hold of my arm, spinning me round to face him. "Seems like unlikely weather for loitering," he said.

Rain dripped from the peak of his cap and fell onto his long nose. The droplets clung to his nostrils with impressive determination before resigning to gravity.

"Doesn't it just," I replied. "Hence why we were on our way home."

"And where is home?"

"At the moment? Hyle Road Safehouse."

"Then you're a very long way from home."

I nodded, sending a shower of drips from my hood. "Just got a little lost. This is our first time in Kumonayo."

"I'd say you got a lot more than a little lost."

"Then a lot lost. That's why we're going. Quickly."

"One problem." His hand moved towards his stun gun. I knew exactly what those things could do, and I certainly didn't want to find myself writhing on the floor with bodily fluids pouring out of me.

I instinctively raised my hands. "We just want to get back and into a dry set of clothes."

"We've had reports of a pair of traders loitering outside that block. And not just today either. What exactly are you looking for?"

"Absolutely nothing. Just admiring the architecture."

"Don't mess me around."

"Look, I thought that somebody I knew lived here, but I've now decided that I was mistaken. We won't be back. In fact, we're leaving Kumonayo first thing tomorrow. Right?"

I nudged Malia, and she nodded in agreement, her hood slipping from her head. She caught it halfway, but it had already revealed her for what she was.

"You're not a trader at all," the warden said. His hand settled on the handle of his stun gun. He shot a look at me. "Do you have papers for her?"

"Back at the safehouse... somewhere..."

"You're coming with me. It's an offence to transport an unregistered carrier into, or out of, city limits. You know that." He eyed me closely. "What's a trader doing with a carrier anyway?"

"She was a birthday present," I said, with more venom than I'd intended.

He slammed me against a building before I even realised he was moving. My head scraped against the wall as his arm pressed across the back of my shoulders. With his other hand, he twisted my arm behind my back. My knees bent in reflex, and I found myself kneeling on the wet ground.

My hands were cuffed and he hauled me back to my feet.

"We didn't have to do this the hard way," he hissed into my ear.

"And miss out on this intimate moment?"

"Do I need to remind you that I'm armed?" He didn't. I wasn't going to forget that. But the anger just kept pouring out of me uncontrollably.

"You wouldn't care about missing papers if I was a merchant. If I didn't have scars you wouldn't have even asked."

"Your kind are in the colonies for a reason. Rats belong out there, scrubbing an existence in the slums. They do not belong in the city, harassing law-abiding citizens. If I had my way you'd all be strung up by the necks."

I clamped my mouth closed.

"I could do it right now and no one would even care. No one would ever ask about you. I'd be hailed a hero if anyone found out. Why do you suppose the authorities let the rogues run free?" He shoved me towards the curb. "Here's our ride."

An auto-car, branded up in police colours, stopped next to us. The warden pulled the back door open and pushed me inside. Malia came next, and finally, he clambered in with us. He pulled the door shut, and the car pulled away, the route to the police station already pre-set.

32

KIOTO

The holding cell was already busy; people of all sorts forced together in one horrible situation. All eyes were on me as I was uncuffed and pushed inside, Malia behind me.

"How long are we going to be in here?" I asked the warden.

He shrugged. "Until they call you for questioning."

"How long is that likely to be?"

He smiled. "I'd make myself comfortable, if I were you."

I wasn't the only trader here. Two more were huddled in one corner: safety in numbers. But Malia's twitching had got worse on the journey here, so we sat as far from anyone else as we could, and turned our backs to them. I took Malia's hands in mine.

"You need to try and fight the shivers," I said. "You need to keep quiet."

She nodded, the strain already evident on her face.

I looked around. "I'm sorry, I just don't know what else to do. Maybe if I had some sleeping pills..."

"It's alright. I'll do my best."

"Hopefully we'll get called soon."

Malia looked at me, her eyes wide. "What will happen to me? Because you have no papers."

"The Arukumbi aren't all carriers. A lot of your people still live free lives—"

"Banished to the marshes in the north," Malia cut in.

"If you're not a slave, you don't need any documents."

"Yes I do. Arukumbi need to carry ID documents with them at all times. Your freedom is very different to mine. Besides, as soon as they realise I have the shivers—"

"Hopefully we'll be out of here before they do."

Malia grunted as she twitched again. "I'm sorry," she said.

"We really need to get out of here soon."

"What are we going to do about finding your sister?" She swallowed hard. "Find her!" she called out.

I didn't need to look up to know that everyone was staring.

"I'm sorry," she whispered. "The memories kind of hook up with things I'm thinking or experiencing."

"I know, I know. It's not your fault. I think we need to find out if this name and the address attached to them is true. Or if, maybe, it used to be true, but isn't anymore. It's been ten years since Omori was taken."

"You'll never find her," Malia said. She shook her head. "Sorry, that wasn't me either."

I nodded and patted her hand. "Someone in this city must know Omori. She must have gone to school, she must have friends. They can't keep her locked up."

"The thing is, are we going to be able to access the right people?"

"We'll just start at the exchange. Maybe her family used a trader once. It's a bloody long shot, but it's all I've got right now. I guess maybe government records... But the chances of me accessing them are slim."

"You'll never find her," Malia repeated, louder this time. "If only Tian were still with us."

"Yeah." I looked down at the floor.

"I'm sorry, I didn't mean to upset you. You two got pretty close, despite... you know."

"Being mortal enemies? Yeah, yeah we did."

"Have you ever heard from him again? After that one time?"

"No. I've had no response to my messages, and every time I try to call him it cuts straight off."

"He's dead!" Malia shouted. "You killed him!"

"What's going on?" A warden was at the door, his hand hovering over his stun gun.

"She's just scared," I said. "She gets nightmares."

"When she's awake?"

"She's just scared," I said again.

"Keep the noise down."

"I'm sorry," Malia whispered.

"It's ok."

"He's coming for you!" The words came out in a scream along with a convulsion that threw her to the floor.

The warden was back at the door, his stun gun in his hand.

"What's going on?"

"Can we just get questioned? You can see that being here is freaking her out."

He squinted in at us. "That's more than her being scared. What's wrong with her?"

"Nothing, really, I'll keep her quiet."

"Maybe I can keep her quiet." He passed his gun from one hand to the other, and then back again.

I held a hand up to him. "No, really, she's fine, I'll keep her quiet."

"I'm so sorry," Malia said again. "The stress is making it worse."

I dropped my head into my hands and thought for a moment, alone, in the darkness. I looked up. "I'm going to have to do an extraction."

"You can't. You know what will happen. If it causes a rush, you'll die."

"If that warden decides to put goodness knows

how many volts into you, you could die. I don't have a choice."

"But I do. I won't let you do this. I was taught how to block a merchant from my head."

"Merchants are very different to traders. Their training is completely different. Their methods, their skill, everything. I'm doing this, and if you try to stop me, it just makes the chance of a rush even greater."

"I don't believe you," she said hesitantly.

I grinned. "Want to take the risk?"

"Screw you," Malia whispered. "What choice do I have?"

"I'll be really gentle. I need you to sit still and quiet. Don't try to fight it at all. Just let me in. We need to do this quickly."

I placed my hand on her forehead and closed my eyes. I tested my way into her head, as if I were walking over a frozen lake. I pushed gently, felt my way around. And then I began to pull, lightly, like unthreading a knitted jumper. It came easily, too easily, and I had to slow down again, fight my sense of urgency. I continued to unravel the memories, taking more and more.

I could feel them coming faster, like a dam about to burst. My head was getting heavier, my thoughts becoming foggy. I pulled my hand away, breaking the connection.

33

SENETSU

The pillow slowly lifted from the back of my head. I stayed on my stomach, my face pressed into the bed.

"What are you doing under there?" asked Saji.

"Trying to find silence," I mumbled.

The bed sank as he sat next to me and placed his hand on my back.

"Omori's playing outside."

"Oblivious." I rolled over and looked up at him. "She's so strangely happy here, and I can't stop asking myself if she's happy because this is a nice place, or if she's just happy because of the extraction and she doesn't know any different. Which means, are we unhappy just because we remember Okaporo, and Kioto, and..." My voice gave out and I wiped a tear from my cheek. "I miss her so much, Saji."

He pulled me up into his arms, wrapping them around me and squeezing me tight.

I closed my eyes and breathed in the scent of him; the comforting smell of earth, and animals, and hard work. My heart ached in my chest, the pain swimming through my body.

"I know, I know," he said soothingly.

"I need to get her back," I said. "I can't be without her anymore."

"We will. We'll go and get her. We'll take Omori and leave Kumonayo far behind us."

"Thank you, thank you. I can't take this anymore." I pulled back from him. "The whispering. The constant whispering. It says Kioto's name over and over. It talks about Okaporo. Some days I swear I can hear their screams in it."

Saji nodded. "I hear it too."

"I asked Tokai about it. And she was so flippant. Told me it was nothing but the wind in the long grass. That the Arukumbi used to call this whole area 'The Whispers'. She said that they believed the whispers were the voices of their ancestors. They'd sit and listen to them for hours, trying to find truths in the sound. Can you imagine that? Can you imagine how crazy that would make you? She said we're not so superstitious, so sentimental to believe such things. That it's nothing but the wind, and we hear in it whatever we want to hear. But I see it, I see it in everyone's eyes. They all know it's far more than that."

34

KIOTO

Slowly, I opened my eyes. The light in the cell was painfully bright. I screwed my eyes shut again, but the pain was already in, behind my eyelids. I pressed my hand to my head.

"Are you alright?" Malia asked. I could feel her hands on me, but it felt disconnected, distant.

"The throw," was all I managed to say.

And then there were hands everywhere, all over me, clasping my arms, pulling me to my feet. I heard Malia say something, but I didn't catch what it was. And then I was walking, or stumbling at least, and there was light and pain and black spots in my vision. And then there was a chair, and a table, and a voice.

I stared at my hands in my lap, my eyes averted

ANGELINE TREVENA

from the lights above me. I stared, and frowned, and tried to keep them in focus.

And then there were questions, and they kept coming. I thought I might be answering, but I had little knowledge of what I was saying. I only hoped that it wasn't the truth.

"Where's Malia?" I asked.

"What?" the voice asked in reply.

"Where's Malia?"

"The carrier?"

"She's not a carrier. She's Arukumbi, but she's not a slave. I'm a trader. We don't have slaves."

"Yes, we thought that was a little curious too. And you don't have any papers for her."

"She's not a—"

A hand was slammed down on the table, and the sound hit me as if that warden had used their stun gun. My brain spun, my vision went dark, and I swallowed back a throat full of hot vomit.

"You've already told me she's a smudger. I just want to know where you got her."

Damn. "She used to be. I bought her, and I freed her. I meant that she used to be a smudger."

"You know that the process doesn't work like that. Her freedom needs to be processed by the courts. She needs to be assessed as fit and healthy. We can't have carriers roaming all over the country unchecked."

"Why are you keeping us?"

"I simply want to know what you were doing outside that block for three days."

"I was looking for someone."

"Your sister."

Again. Damn. "I really don't feel well."

"We're not playing that one. What are you doing in Kumonayo, Kioto? You're a hell of a long way from home."

"I have no home."

"A trader without roots? I find that hard to believe."

"My roots were burnt," I said.

"What does that mean?"

I sighed. "I'm from Okaporo."

Even through my pounding head, I could hear the intake of breath. It was always the same reaction. People liked to give themselves a moment to consider what to say next.

"And where have you been since then?"

I sighed again. "Kagosaka until I was 16. And then, just wherever my feet took me."

"And where did you come across this smudger?"

"I don't remember."

"Really." It was an accusation rather than a question.

"I've been all over the place. Everywhere kind of looks the same after a while."

"Then let's try why you have her."

"She seemed nice."

"She seemed nice?"

"Yes. I wanted to free her. Have you never done anything nice for someone?"

I risked raising my eyes a little. I could see his

hands on the table between us. His neat, clean nails. His crisp, white shirt cuffs, the crease ironed into the sleeve. His expensive watch. His wedding ring. All lit in that sickly green glow that showed he had a screen open, floating somewhere between his head and mine. Recording me.

"So you picked up this smudger, but you don't remember where, simply because you wanted to do something nice? How much did you pay for her? Do you remember that?"

"I don't, no."

"For a trader, someone who deals in memories, who probes through other people's heads, your memory isn't very impressive, is it?"

I shrugged. "Perhaps it's all that childhood trauma."

"I can keep you here for a very long time, if that's how you want to play it."

"I'd like that, the hospitality has been top notch."

"I'm glad you find it all so amusing. You know that I can hold traders for five days before I need to petition for longer. And do you know how many of those petitions are denied?"

"I can't think."

"None. Not one. Ever. And, as for your carrier, I can detain her indefinitely. I can return her to her former owner if I wish. Or I could have her destroyed."

My eyes flicked up to rest on his stubbled chin. They ached at the strain, and I dropped my gaze back to my lap.

"You didn't know that, did you? She's property, nothing more. Until her freedom is granted by the courts, not by you, she's no more alive to me than this table. And I can have her destroyed just like that."

We sat in silence for a moment.

"Maybe that helps your memory a little?" he suggested.

The door opened, the thud of it rattling through my skull, and another body entered the room. There was whispering, shuffling, scraping, more footsteps.

"Excuse me."

And then I was alone. And I was alone for a long time. Enough time for the symptoms of the throw to recede to a dull ache in my sinuses, and a slight discomfort in my stomach. Enough time for me to run through every moment of the conversation, to analyse every word, every gesture, every silence. Enough time for my confidence to fall apart, and for me to imagine awful, horrible outcomes. All of the worst case scenarios, and scenarios even worse than those.

I shook my head to try and clear it, the unfamiliar memories jingling around like bells. I started pushing them backwards, filing them away somewhere they wouldn't bother me too much. But one of them snagged, it didn't want to move. This memory was something different. It clung on because it recognised my own memories. It recognised me. It was one of Omori's.

I cradled it like I'd once cradled my new born baby sister; so scared of dropping it if I didn't hold on tightly enough, but equally scared of hurting it if I hung on too tightly. It was so precious, and I vowed to protect it with my life, just as I had when Omori was born.

And then the door opened again. I looked up.

"You're free to go."

35

SENETSU

As I walked towards the community hut, I looked over at the merchant's wagon parked outside Tokai's house. It wasn't the first one I'd seen in the colony.

The community hut was almost empty. It was late, and most people had already eaten. They were all back at home, tucking their children into bed.

Saji was tucking Omori in tonight. I couldn't stand her bright eyes and broad smile anymore. I was swollen with guilt for feeling that way, but every time she told me how happy she was, it was as if she'd slapped me around the face. I could only see it as being smug, triumphant, conceited. It was wrong, it was disgusting that I felt that way. I hated her. No. I hated myself. I hated everything that had happened, and everything that we'd done.

I served myself a plate of food, dried out under the hot lights. I sat apart from anyone else. I knew I was meant to be trying to integrate, to make this place, at least, some kind of home, but I couldn't look anyone in the eye tonight.

My solitude was quickly interrupted, however, as Tokai settled herself across the table from me.

"It's nice to see you in here, even if you are sitting alone," she said.

I nodded, and shovelled a large forkful of potato into my mouth.

"How are you all settling in?"

I cocked my head from side to side, weighing up my answer. "Omori's very happy here, she's always telling me so."

"That can't be easy."

"It's not. I mean, I'm glad she's happy, we only ever want to see our children happy, don't we?"

"And children are so strong, so adaptable. Not like us. We hold onto things. Old feelings, old memories. Things that no longer serve us. Things that hurt us even. For no reason other than sentimentality."

"Isn't it important to remember the past?"

"Not if it's to the detriment of your present."

"But we remember our ancestors."

Tokai nodded. "We remember them for their wise words. Wise words that help us live our lives, help us move forward. We don't remember them so that we can spend our lives looking backwards."

I stared at my food. I hadn't come here to be scolded like a child.

"Why is there a merchant wagon outside your house?" I asked.

Tokai shrugged. "Just business."

"What business could merchants possibly have in a colony?"

"We're all doing the same thing, Senetsu. It makes little sense to be fighting against one another all the time. Life is a lot easier for everyone if we collaborate instead. It's common sense, really."

"And what about the carriers they leave behind?"

Tokai shook her head slightly. "What carriers?"

"I've heard them, calling out in the night. It sounds like the shivers. What do you want with smudgers?"

Tokai smiled and patted my hand which was fisted around my knife. "I don't have any smudgers. I never have. The merchants don't leave any carriers here. What would I possibly want with them?"

I frowned. "I don't know."

"It's just the stress of everything. Last week you were hearing Kioto's name on the wind."

"Something is not right here," I hissed. I scraped back my chair, stood, and walked out.

I turned towards our house, but I found myself striding past it, out into the hills. I stood and faced the wind, held my breath, and listened.

36

KIOTO

I frowned. "What?"

"You're free to go."

I stood up quickly, afraid that they might change their minds. I looked at the officer as I passed him. His eyes gave nothing away. I wondered what it might be like being married to someone like that. Someone that didn't open up, someone that kept themselves so hidden.

"I suggest you cut your stay in Kumonayo as short as you can," he said. "I don't want to see you again."

I stepped into the corridor beyond, and the air seemed impossibly fresh. The light, offered up by the same fizzing electric lights as inside the interrogation room, seemed softer, friendlier, more welcoming.

"Where's Malia?" I asked.

"She's being released with you." He pointed down the corridor. "They'll sign you out at reception."

I could hear the sharpness in his voice. Whoever had decided that we could leave, it wasn't him.

I glanced back as I walked the way he had pointed. Something wasn't right, but whatever had happened, I was going to take advantage of it. I glanced upwards and whispered "thank you" to the High.

The reception was large, light, and busy. It looked more like a shopping centre than a police station. There were even a couple of convenience stores along one side, in case you were stuck here long enough to need a magazine and a chocolate fix.

We hadn't been brought in this way. They didn't want the common criminals mixing with the general public. But I was a free woman now, apparently cleared of all suspicions of wrongdoing.

I looked around for Malia. She was stood at the counter, talking to a warden behind the desk. I hurried over.

As I stepped up next to her, I shot her a smile. She smiled back, her eyes sharply focussed on me.

I turned to the warden. "I'm told I need to sign out here?"

The warden sighed and, with his tongue pushed into his cheek, tapped a screen already drawn out on the counter. It flickered slightly as he touched it.

"Sign here."

I touched the screen, but my finger passed straight through it.

He sighed again. "No implants. Use that." He gestured to a screen pen that dangled from the desk at the end of a short chain.

The screen had a substance under the pen's nib, albeit a little jelly-like. I attempted my signature, but it came out wonky and illegible.

The warden touched the screen again. "Sign here as receipt of your belongings."

"I didn't have any belongings."

He sighed once more and spun the screen to face him. "They collected your things from your given home address. Hyle Road Safehouse. It was confiscated and searched as evidence."

"Oh right. Thanks."

He spun the screen back around and I signed my name again. He ran a cyber card over the screen, and it disappeared.

"Take this to evidence dispatch to collect your belongings." He lazily pointed across the reception, his arm barely rising above the desk.

I linked my arm into Malia's and followed his vague direction.

"Are you ok?" I asked.

"Fine. You?"

"That was horrible. I had the throw through most of it, really bad too. I'm not entirely certain of what I said, but definitely some things I hadn't intended to. But..." I shrugged, "we're in the clear, so it can't have been that bad."

"Doesn't it seem a bit suspicious? Them suddenly letting us go like that?"

"Hugely so, but I'm not going to stand around questioning it until we're a long way from here."

"Good plan."

We arrived at the evidence dispatch desk and I handed my cyber card to a warden who looked as bored and fed up as the one we'd just spoken to. Maybe it was a condition of employment.

She hefted my bag up onto the counter, and I took it from her.

"Thank you," I said, but received nothing more than a grunt in reply.

"Let's get out of here," I said to Malia.

We stepped out into the cool air of sunset, the lights of the city bleeding an acrid orange into the sky. There might have been a beautiful sunset, offering an alternative display of pinks and purples, but you'd never know.

"Where to?" Malia asked.

"Well, I guess we can't go back to the safehouse, and we're certainly not welcome back at the colony, and we'd better avoid Omori's home for a while. In fact, laying low for a few days isn't too bad an idea."

"So, somewhere we can squat?"

I nodded. "I guess so. Hopefully before it gets too cold and dark. How are you feeling now?"

"Better. Lighter."

"Good."

"But what about you?"

I waved a dismissive hand at her. "Don't worry

about me, this is what I'm trained to do. My choice. You never had that luxury. Maybe we can do this every now and again. Gently pull some of your memories out. Until you're all empty of them."

"We need to get rid of those first," Malia said, pointing at my head.

"Yep, and smudges aren't always easy to find a buyer for."

"I can't understand why anyone would ever want to buy a bad memory."

"Well, there are lots of reasons. And a memory that's sad for one person, isn't necessarily sad for someone else. Like, sometimes, it's better to have a memory of a painful break up, rather than living with the truth that no one's ever loved you. I once sold a bunch of failed business memories to someone who was setting up in business for the first time, because they wanted to have some experiences to learn from. Then there are people who enjoy bad memories. 'Smudge rubbers' we call them."

"What do you mean, they enjoy them?"

"Because they can live out their fantasies. Like someone who's weak might like to have a memory of beating someone up, so that they can pretend to themselves that they really did it. Or someone who's timid might like a memory of having a blazing row in public, or doing something very risqué, or breaking the law. Things like that."

Malia grimaced. She'd spent years subjected to such violent and unhappy memories.

"I know," I said. "It's weird and twisted, but

that's how the world is. And if it lets us get rid of these smudges, then so be it."

"I guess."

I spun round as someone called out my name. A man was striding towards us, his hand raised as if he might be waving. But it wasn't a friendly wave. His clothes, his close-cropped hair, the feather tied to his shirt. I knew straight away what he was. He was a rogue.

37

KIOTO

I grabbed Malia's wrist and, without explanation, set off at a run, dragging her behind me.

She stumbled, falling against me, but I managed to keep us both upright.

"What's happening?" she gasped.

I stopped, almost tripping over my own feet, as another two rogues appeared ahead. I turned, but there were more behind us. I twisted, pulling Malia with me, tried to find a gap, but there were hands all over us, and those hands were strong, and the arms that followed were strong, and their legs pressed into the backs of our knees to force us to the ground.

An auto-car pulled up, a real automated drive one, not a filthy petrol hybrid like they usually drove.

We were pushed into the back seat, and other bodies piled in behind us, pinning us in. The engine hummed, and the car started to move.

I squeezed Malia's hand and leaned in close to her. "I'll keep you safe, don't worry."

She nodded quickly.

We didn't travel for long, placing us well within the city limits still. We were dragged from the car, pulled down some steps, and pushed through a door. And then we were left there, alone.

We were stood in a basement room. The walls were bare brick, the low ceiling exposed the beams that supported the floor above. Bare light bulbs quivered at the ends of their wires as feet tramped about upstairs. The door behind us had been closed, and an open archway offered a view of nothing but darkness ahead. Besides a small stack of chairs in one corner, the room was empty.

"You ok?" I asked Malia.

She nodded once, and her hand tightened in mine.

"Who are they?" she said.

"Rogues."

"Are they going to kill us?"

"Not if I can help it."

A rogue entered the room through the archway. He walked straight towards us, purposefully, and I stepped forward, putting myself between him and Malia. He stopped in front of me and held out his hand.

I stared at it.

"It's traditional to shake it," he said.

I looked up at him. "It's also traditional for your kind to kill my kind, so excuse me if I'm a little standoffish."

He nodded. "Fair enough." He withdrew his offered hand. "I'm Dai, the leader of this bunch of losers and outcasts. And you are Kioto."

"Well done."

"But I don't know who this is." He peered past me at Malia.

"She is none of your business," I said.

He shrugged. "Ok. But you are. As is your sister."

"My sister's dead."

"Don't play that game. I know she's alive, and I know that you know she's alive. And that you're looking for her. You see, I don't need to crawl around inside people's heads to know everything that goes on in this city. I knew the moment you arrived, and we've been watching you ever since."

"So, if you know everything, why don't you have my sister already? Why grab me? I'm nothing to you."

"Because this isn't my operation."

I eyed him. "So who's pulling your strings?"

"Someone you might know."

He stepped to one side to reveal a figure stood in the archway. I blinked. It couldn't be true. I walked forward several steps.

"You're dead," I said.

Narata shook her head. "Apparently not."

"How did you get out of Okaporo?"

She stepped forward and took hold of my hands.

"After I sent your parents away with Omori, I got myself out."

I tore my hands from hers. "And you left everyone behind to die? You were our brood mother, you were meant to protect us."

"There was just no time, Kioto. The rogues were upon us. I didn't have time to get anyone else out."

"So you just walked out and left them? You only thought about saving yourself." I looked back at Dai. "And what are you doing here? With them?"

Narata walked past me to stand with the rogue. "I've known Dai since I was a child. We grew up together. You know that, when I was eight, I was taken from my colony as part of the Liberation Scheme. But, as I had already had my trader scars, no family wanted to adopt me, so I spent the rest of my childhood in one of their orphanages. Not that that's really what it was. All of those children had parents who loved and missed us desperately. I met Dai there, and we grew so close. We were inseparable. He's like a brother to me."

"A rogue?"

"He wasn't a rogue then. He was just another child stolen from the colonies."

"But he's a rogue now."

"He is."

"And he's still like a brother to you. Despite everything. Despite what his people—"

"They weren't my people," Dai said.

I didn't even look at him. I kept my eyes locked on Narata's. "Did..." I swallowed. "Did you tell the rogues what Omori was? Did you tell them that the vessel was in Okaporo?"

Narata gripped me hard by the shoulders. "No. Absolutely not."

"How can I trust anything you say now? You walked out of your own colony and left your own people to die. And then you stayed hidden for eleven years, pretending that you were dead. Have you got any idea what I've been through? How much I needed you?" I couldn't hold the tears back anymore. They flowed hot and fast over my cheeks. I wiped them away angrily.

"I'm sorry, Kioto. But you have to believe me, I did not cause what happened in Okaporo. If I could have saved everyone, of course I would. Every single life that was lost that night, I've carried that weight in my heart ever since. I'm so sorry. And it was only because of Dai that I managed to get your parents and Omori out. If he hadn't... They would have died there too."

"They're dead anyway."

She nodded slowly. "I heard. And I'm so sorry." Her hand rose to her chest.

I grabbed hold of her wrist and threw her arm aside. "No. Don't," I said. "Don't you dare do that. Don't you dare pretend you give a shit."

"Omori is still alive. And that's because of everything we've done to protect her. I got her out of Okaporo in time. I went into hiding, let everyone believe that I was dead, all to protect her whereabouts. And Tokai, whose trust I put her into, she protected her too."

"If you can call tearing her away from everything she belonged to 'protecting her'. And what about me? For eleven years I've thought that my whole family were dead. Thought that you were dead. I found out by accident. Were you ever going to reappear to tell me the truth?"

"You had your own life to lead, and a new home in Kagosaka. I knew that you would be safe. Looked after. And look at you, you've flourished."

"I wasn't looked after at all. None of us were. We were treated like outsiders every single day we were there. They also refused to train us properly. We had to have secret lessons every evening with the Okaporo rooks. It was never a home. They hated us. That's what you left us to. We were children."

"I thought you'd be happy there. I didn't know I was leaving you to that."

"You left us. Regardless of what you thought you were leaving us to, you still left us."

"But you've done alright." Her voice was barely more than a whimper.

"I left Kagosaka on the morning of my 16th birthday. I haven't been back since. I did alright by myself. All alone."

"Have you been back to...?" She left the question unfinished.

"No. I haven't been back to the coast at all. I've not seen the ocean in years. I lost everything," I said coldly.

"I thought I was doing the right thing."

"You couldn't have been more wrong."

Dai cleared his throat. "It's been a long, confusing day. I think we all need to get some sleep, and see how things look in the morning."

Only then did I realise how exhausted I was. The only thing that had been keeping me going was anger, and that was quickly fading into a shadowy sense of regret. This woman, my brood mother, I'd respected and admired her while she was alive, and I'd practically deified her since her assumed death. The reality was a very poor second to my memories of her.

"My whole life has been a lie," I said, "and I don't see how one night is going to change any of that."

38

SENETSU

I was in the middle of cooking when Tokai arrived. The kitchen was filled with steam that clung to the walls like sweat. My sleeves were rolled up, my face flushed.

Saji had barely opened the front door to her before she marched into the kitchen. She gripped the back of one of the dining chairs and stared straight at me.

"Good evening, Tokai," I said without a smile. "You've caught us in the middle of family time."

"We keep an open door policy here, no matter what time of day."

"Of course. And it's always open to you. Would you like to join us?" I gestured towards the bubbling pans. "It won't be too long now."

"No, thank you. I take my meals in the hut, surrounded by my friends." Everything she said was laced with half-submerged hostility.

"Then, what can we do for you?"

"I came to discuss Omori's training. I've found a suitable rook for her, and she'll be starting her lessons next week."

"But she's only just turned five."

"I'm sure that you can understand that Omori is a very special girl. Her training will be far more complex, more challenging. It's also far more vital. We decided that it would be in everyone's best interests to start training her early."

"Who's 'we'? Because perhaps her parents should have been involved in that discussion."

Tokai bowed her head. "The training of Kumonayo children is a matter for the whole community. As representatives for that community, we took the weight of this difficult decision upon ourselves."

"Don't do that. Don't make it sound so selfless of you. This wasn't some kind of burden. This is you doing what's best for you. Not best for us, and certainly not best for Omori."

"It is my job, as brood mother—"

"You're not our brood mother."

"Like it or not, I am now. Okaporo is gone, and Narata with it. She put you into our care, and we've taken you in despite the terrible danger that's put this colony in."

"You want the vessel as much as anyone else. The danger is more than worth it to you."

"Whatever your thoughts on it, the decision has been made. Omori's training will begin as planned."

I looked at Saji. He crossed the kitchen and stood beside me.

"Then we'll leave," he said. "We'll take Omori, and we'll go and get Kioto."

"Don't be ridiculous," Tokai said. "The world is crawling with rogues that want to see you all dead."

"We made it here just fine."

"You made it here on pure luck."

"We've already lost one daughter. You're not taking our other one away too."

Tokai tossed her head. "Don't be so dramatic. I'm not taking her anywhere, we're simply starting her training a year early. Honestly, you people."

I slipped my hand into Saji's. "We're going to walk out of here tomorrow, and you can't stop us," I said.

"You're right, I can't. You're not prisoners here. But you have no idea of the layers of protection this place has."

"You mean all of your little secrets?"

"Little secrets that keep your daughter safe."

"Only one of them," said Saji. "Our minds are made up."

"Kioto has a life of her own now. She's being trained in Kagosaka, and I hear that she's settled in well there. If you turn up, you'll put her progress back by years. You'll upset her entire future. Is that what you want? She thinks that you're dead. She's mourned for you, she's said goodbye. Do you really want to throw her entire life, her entire future, up into the air like that?"

"She's better off with us," I said, silently cursing the emotional crack in my voice.

Tokai grabbed it. "You're not thinking clearly. When you wake up in the morning you'll see that this makes sense. That this is the best thing you can do for both of your daughters."

"We should never have come here."

Tokai threw her hands up in the air. "Fine. Leave. These hills are crawling with rogues, and it's my little 'secrets' that keep them at bay. Just see how long you last out there alone. Because once you step out of the colony I cannot protect you anymore, and I will not be responsible for whatever fate finds you."

39

KIOTO

We were given a bedroom upstairs; a proper room, with a proper bed. I'd expected a mattress on the floor of a damp basement room, but Dai kept pointing out that we weren't prisoners. He only asked that we stayed long enough to hear what he had to say.

In fact, we'd been offered two rooms, but we'd both said, without hesitation, that we'd share. The double bed was large and luxurious, and by lying on either side of it, it felt like there had been a void between us. We'd gotten used to sharing single beds in safehouses, or huddling together for warmth in barns.

We woke to sunlight filtered through the white curtains, and the sounds of the city outside. But not the parts of the city we were more used to waking up to. I heard no sirens, no drunken shouting, no screams, no cursing. It was just the hum of auto-cars, and the sounds of normal, everyday people waking up to their normal, everyday lives.

I sat up and looked at Malia, who was still sleeping soundly. I quietly dressed, and then went in search of the kitchen.

It was easy enough to find by the smell of bacon and cooking oil that hung heavy in the air. There was only one other person in there; a rogue probably only a few years older than me. He was sat, cross legged, on a worktop, eating a bacon sandwich. He nodded to me, his mouth full of food.

I didn't respond. I spotted a coffee machine and started opening cupboards to find some mugs.

"Wanna hand?" he asked, slipping down to the floor. "It's not very well laid out in here. Not very intuitive. You'll never find anything by yourself."

Behind the fourth cupboard door I opened, I finally found mugs. I held one up to him. "I'm fine."

"Ok." He hopped back up onto the worktop. "You're Kioto," he said.

"How observant of you."

"Dai's been following you for a while. I could teach you some stuff about covering your tracks, if you like."

"I'm fine, thanks."

I poured myself a coffee and splashed in a tiny bit of milk. I needed the boost this morning.

"You're not very friendly, are you?"

I shrugged and turned away from him.

"So, I heard that you're pretty good at what you do. I also heard that you're from Okaporo. And that you've got a smudger. I've never met a trader with a carrier before."

I looked back at him. "I'm surprised you hear anything at all, seeing as you never actually stop talking."

He nodded with a smile. "Not a morning person, eh?"

"Actually, I am a morning person. Just not a rogue person. Making small talk with a ruthless killer isn't my idea of fun."

"I've never killed anyone. Well, unless you count house plants. I'm not very green fingered."

"Is this a joke to you?"

He laughed. "Is what a joke?"

"Okaporo? What your kind have been doing to traders for generations?"

He held his hands up. "Be careful, that chip on your shoulder is growing even bigger. It must be hard work having to carry that around with you all day."

I stared at him.

"Ok, still a touchy subject then. Do you know why I'm a rogue? Because my mum is. I was born into it, and I've never known anything different. I've never met a trader, or a carrier, or even a merchant before. But I've learnt about them all. And I'm sorry about what's happened to you, but it has nothing to do with me. You look at me, and all you see is a killer. I would have thought that a trader, of all people, would be less quick to judge seeing as everyone just looks at you and sees your scars. That's all you are to them. But that's not fair, there's a lot more to you, right? Yet you look at me, and you do exactly the same thing."

"That's different."

"How?"

"Because I do it as a survival instinct. Not just because I'm prejudiced."

"And what am I going to do? Beat you to death with my bacon sandwich?"

"I'm sure you have a knife hidden somewhere. Or a gun."

He patted himself down. "Damn, must've left it in my other jeans."

"I'm glad this is funny to you."

He shoved the last bite of his breakfast into his mouth and spoke through it, with half a crust protruding.

"Why've you got a carrier anyway? I thought you guys didn't agree with that."

"I don't agree with it. She's not a slave."

"So, what is she? Your pet?"

"She's a human being. She's my friend."

He frowned at me. "Are you always this serious?"

Tian's face flew into my mind then. I tried to push it away, but the image persisted. I couldn't work out what annoyed me more; the fact that this rogue reminded me of Tian, or the fact that I really liked that he did. I shook my head, and managed to dislodge the thoughts with the motion.

"Good morning, Kioto," said Dai, walking in. "Did

you sleep well?"

"Well enough"

"I hope you're not bothering our guest, Finch. And get off there, that's so unhygienic."

The boy uncrossed his legs and slid off the worktop.

"Don't call me that," he said. "At least shorten it to 'Fire'."

Dai gave him a stern look. "Firefinch. Your presence is no longer required. Go and find somewhere else to be."

With a glance at Kioto, Firefinch loped out of the kitchen.

"Can I make you something to eat?" Dai asked. "Or do traders survive on coffee alone?"

"I'll have whatever's going," I said.

"Sit down then." He gestured to the small dining table.

I sat down and watched him busy himself.

"How can you go from being a colony trader, to being a rogue?" I asked him.

He stopped moving and stood with his back to me, his head bowed.

"I don't remember the colony much. I was taken from there when I was three. I don't really remember my parents. I have nothing that ties me to the colonies. I don't even know which one I was taken from."

"What about your blood? That ties you to the colonies."

"My blood?" He turned and looked at me. "No

one ever came looking for me. So my blood obviously didn't mean very much."

"But your roots..." I didn't bother finishing the sentence. I could barely lecture someone on the importance of clinging onto your roots. It was the foundation of the trader culture, and I'd turned my back on all of my roots. I closed my eyes and tried to imagine the sound of the sea. Once upon a time, the sound of the waves was as familiar to me as the sound of my own breathing.

He placed a plate, brimming with fried food, in front of me. Then he sat in the chair opposite.

"Are you going to watch me eat?" I asked.

"I just want to talk to you. About your sister."

"I can't help you. I don't know anything about my sister. I don't even know where she lives."

"You do. You had exactly the right building."

I leaned forward. "Have you seen her?"

"Many times. She looks like you."

"What do you want with her?"

Dai looked at me intensely. He let the silence hang for a moment. "Do you know what she is?"

I nodded quickly.

"Once upon a time vessels were rare, oddities, genetic mutations. They showed up about once every other generation. Just one. Here or there. Easy to track down. But now, there are lots."

"Lots? What do you mean, lots?"

Your generation, we know of at least eighty having been born."

I whistled. "I had no idea."

"Not many people do. We've even met a merchant vessel, and that's never, ever happened before. The traders are doing what they can to keep it quiet. You realise how many people would want to get their hands on a vessel. You know what carrying other people's memories for too long can do to you. Your friend certainly knows it. To have someone you can just pour memories into, someone they just flow straight out of, like a drain, that's worth a lot. Even more if people realise how rare it is."

"But the rogues are hunting them down to kill them, aren't they? I mean, aren't you?"

He leaned back in his chair. "Yes. I am."

"You admit it, just like that. Like admitting you broke a mug?"

"You don't know what these vessels can do, Kioto. They're not just someone to offload unwanted memories into. They've developed, evolved, if you like."

"Evolved how?"

"Look at this." He drew a screen out on the table between us.

"You've got implants?" I asked.

"Couldn't resist." He gestured to the room around us. "As you can see, we're not your traditional band of rogues."

"You've evolved too, huh?"

"Look at this." He spun the screen towards me.

It was a news article, but he gave me no time to read it before he continued.

"Now, you tell me, what would make a man

who's never been in any trouble before, with no strong political leanings, your absolute everyday, average Joe, what would make him wake up one morning and decide to assassinate a reader? A member of the council. What would prompt a man to do something so out of character? His wife says he left for work as normal. But instead of going to work, he went and bought himself an illegal gun. And then he went to the city hall and put four bullets into a reader's head. Explain that."

I looked up at him. "I don't know. People do crazy things all the time. Maybe his wife burnt his breakfast."

"Or maybe someone put the idea in his head."

"What do you mean?"

"This is what the vessels can do. They can implant thoughts, impulses, desires, compulsions. They can make people do whatever they want them to. Just imagine the possibilities of that. They could start wars, genocide, massacres, mass suicides. They could change the political landscape beyond measure. They could influence anyone they wanted in any way that they wished."

"That's ridiculous."

"That's what we thought. But we've been researching this for years, and these kinds of cases are becoming more and more common. What's more, the people being apparently randomly killed, it looks like not only are the vessels doing this, but they're selling their services. They're becoming contract killers."

"I don't believe you."

"You don't have to. All the evidence is here." He tapped the screen. "There's story after story after story like that one." He scrolled through the articles. "You see. There's loads of them."

"But this could be anything. This could be air pollution sending people crazy, or something in their drinking water. Or just the sudden realisation that their lives are totally shit. Don't you ever wake up and wonder what the point is? I know I often wake up wanting to kill someone."

"These aren't random events. I could believe your theory if they killed their spouses, or their neighbour, or even a random stranger who happened to be in the wrong place at the wrong time. But these are people purposefully crossing an entire city to specifically target someone in particular. They aren't random killings, their victims have been chosen."

"By who?"

Dai shrugged. "That, we don't know. Yet. But we've been following these stories, going to where they happened, talking to people. And we've been hunting down vessels. And we've found them almost every time."

I stared at his hands. Hands that dealt out death.

"So if you've known where my sister is, why haven't you just killed her?" My heart seemed to slow as I asked the question, my blood cooling to ice.

"Because we have a job for her."

"But she's not even trained."

"Not yet. But she will be."

"You want her to be trained as a vessel? But she's no danger to anyone right now."

"And she's no use to anyone either. You see, the other thing about vessels is that they're somehow linked. They can find one another. The closer they get to another vessel, the more painful it becomes for them. If they touch another vessel, it can be fatal for them both."

"And you want to use her to find other vessels."

"Exactly." He folded his arms and smiled smugly.

"Not going to happen."

He raised an eyebrow. His arrogance made me want to crawl across the table and scratch his eyes out.

"Because," I continued, "she can't be trained. She doesn't have all of her memories."

"I know."

"You know?"

"Of course. But I have a feeling you know where her missing memories are. You see, I asked myself what a trader would be doing with a carrier. Particularly a smudger, and especially a topped out smudger. Now, there has been a growing trend in traders buying topped out smudgers, but they don't tend to travel the country with them. They get rid of them pretty quickly. Which means your smudger has something valuable in her. Something valuable to you. And, if I'm right, something incredibly valuable to me."

"I don't know what you're talking about."

"Really? Because the look of panic in your eyes

tells me a totally different story." He leaned forward. "I know what she's carrying just as well as you do."

"I'm not going to let you do this."

"You can't stop me."

"Omori's no threat to anyone as long as she's not trained up. Why can't you just leave her alone?"

"And what are you going to do with those memories of hers? Surely you want to give them back. That's why you've brought your smudger all this way."

I calculated things quickly, my thoughts tripping and stumbling over one another.

"Then I'll kill Malia. Omori's memories will die with her."

"I can't let you do that. We want Omori. That means we need Malia. And to bring all of this together, we need you."

"But you said that we weren't your prisoners."

"You're not. You can leave any time you want." He leaned back and laced his hands behind his head. "But if you do, I'll kill you, your smudger, and your sister."

We both turned as Narata cleared her throat in the doorway.

"Dai," she said. "Let me speak with Kioto. Alone."

40

KIOTO

I paced the kitchen as I relayed mine and Dai's conversation to Narata. My hands flew around wildly, and I had no resolve to hold them still. Tears stung the backs of my eyes. I would not cry. I needed to be strong.

Narata grabbed me by the shoulders, giving me a little shake.

"Do you trust me?" she asked.

My mind was a whirlwind; I could barely even trust myself.

"Do you trust me?" she asked again.

"In the last few weeks, everything I thought I knew about my life, about myself, has turned out to be wrong. I don't know what to trust right now."

"You need to trust me, Kioto. Well, really, you have no choice. I am Omori's only hope. Dai trusts me completely, I have his ear, he listens to me. We'll restore Omori's memories, I'll train her, and then I'll get us out of here. I know everything about this place, about these rogues. You wouldn't be able to escape without my help."

"And where would we go? Where would be safe for us?"

"We'll be protected in the colonies, don't worry about that. I'll get us somewhere safe."

"Like Okaporo was safe?"

"Neither you nor your sister died there. I can protect us, Kioto."

"We could rebuild Okaporo," I said. It was a hope I'd never dared speak out loud before, one I'd been carrying for years without the means to satisfy it.

"We could," she agreed. "We will. We'll return to our ancestors."

"The others will return from Kagosaka. I left there three years ago, but I can't imagine anything's changed. They won't need any persuading to return home."

"Then that's what we'll do, as soon as it's safe. We'll rebuild Okaporo with true Okaporo blood."

"I can have a home again," I said slowly, feeling the weight of the idea. "And I can see the sea again."

"But first, I need the memory you're carrying. My ripped memory. The one that brought you here."

"Of course."

I watched as Narata performed the Dedication

with precision and reverence. It was a beautiful performance to watch. Sacred. Far from the rushed version of it I usually made do with. The shame rose in me like nausea.

I sat down, leaning back in the chair, and closed my eyes. I felt Narata's hand lay on my stomach, the other on my forehead.

"You need to help me," Narata whispered. "I can't take it, I need you to give it to me."

I pushed the memory forward. And then further. I didn't simply offer it up for her to take, I pushed it right out of me and into her mind. There was a slight tug, and then the discomfort the scratch had given me was gone.

"It's torn to shreds," Narata said. She shook her head. "It'll take a few days to repair itself. You've been carrying this? It must have been uncomfortable."

"Really uncomfortable. Like sleeping with an acorn under your back."`

"Thank you." She shook her head again, as if trying to shake the memory back into its rightful place. "I haven't been able to practice trading for years. I can't wait to get back to it."

"Who took it from you?" I asked.

"Tokai. She did it to protect Omori. She said that if even I didn't know where I'd sent her, no one could get the information out of me."

"So she had all the power when it came to Omori."

Narata nodded. "She did. But I don't know how

you ended up with this memory. Who did you take it from?"

"It was a rip job. They didn't exactly give me their business card."

"Who were you supposed to deliver it to?"

"I was never given a name. Just an address. In Honporo." I dug into my pockets and handed her the cyber card.

She held it up to the light. "Honporo. Why would this message be going to Honporo?"

"They paid really well for it too. I was meant to get the second half on delivery. I would've got my pebble back too."

"Your pebble?"

"They took it as collateral. It was the only thing I had left from Okaporo. My only link to the only home I've ever known. The only link to my family. I guess I'll lose that now."

"Soon enough, they'll realise you're not going to deliver it too."

"They'll probably come looking for it. A lot rests on this memory. It was made very clear to us how precious it was, and how dangerous it was to be carrying it. We had rogues looking for us."

"Us? You and Malia?"

"Me and Tian. He was carrying the other half. We were meant to be travelling separately, but it didn't quite pan out like that. That's why they'd chosen a trader and a merchant to split it between. They thought we would never want to travel together."

"Tian's a merchant?"

"His mother was a trader. From Miyakata, I guess. His grandparents still lived in the colony."

"How come you ended up with the whole memory?"

"He gave me his half. I only understood what it all meant once I played the whole thing. We had rogues right on top of us. He gave me his half, and then he led the rogues away."

"What happened to him?"

"I don't know. I had one message from him a while later telling me to play the scratch and follow my heart. I've heard nothing from him since."

41

SENETSU

When I opened the door, Tokai was stood on the other side, arms folded, foot tapping impatiently. She pushed past me and stepped into the house.

"What happened to our open door policy, Senetsu?"

"I'm sorry, I guess I forgot."

"I'm told Saji didn't turn up to work this morning. Where is he?"

"That's why I locked the door. I didn't want anyone coming in. He's sick. Really nasty stomach bug, he can't keep anything down. I didn't want anyone else to get it."

Her face didn't look convinced, but she still took a step back towards the open front door.

"Is he in bed?"

"Sleeping, finally. He was up most of the night."

"And how's Omori?"

"She's fine, for now. But you know how stomach bugs are; once one person gets them, they go through the whole family. It's probably best that we just quarantine ourselves for a while."

Tokai grunted. "Maybe I should check in on him, give him my best wishes."

"I'd rather you didn't, like I said, he was up most of the night throwing up. It was really quite violent. The room is a mess, I haven't had a chance to wash the bedsheets yet. I wouldn't want you to catch it. It's knocked him out entirely, and he's a fit, healthy man. I'd hate to see someone more vulnerable get it."

Tokai nodded sharply. "I want to see him back at work as soon as he's better."

"Of course. Saji certainly isn't one to take time off unnecessarily. It's hard enough to get him to take a day off when he is actually ill."

"And Omori's lessons will start as planned."

"Let's hope she doesn't catch it then."

"Perhaps she could stay with one of the other families for a little while. Just to protect her from it, if it's as nasty as you say."

"That would be a great idea, except she might already have it. I don't think either of us want to see it go around the entire colony."

"No." Tokai stared at me for a moment. "Well then, give him my best. I hope he feels better soon."

"I will. Thank you."

I pressed the door closed behind her, and slowly exhaled. It felt like I'd been holding my breath the whole time.

I walked down the short corridor to Omori's room. I stopped on the way to pull mine and Saji's bedroom door closed, concealing the empty room beyond.

"Are you alright, sweetheart?" I asked her, stepping into her room.

"Was Tokai here?" she asked.

"She was. She came to say hello and see how we were settling in."

"I like her."

"I know you do. You've settled here nicely, haven't you?"

"Can I go and play outside?"

"Not today, honey."

"Where's Daddy?"

"Daddy's at work."

"But he left early this morning. And he's not wearing his work boots. They're still in the bathroom."

"He's just doing different work today."

"When's he coming home?"

"It will probably be late. Maybe even after your bedtime."

Omori sighed. "Will he come and say goodnight?"

"I'll make sure of it." I ruffled her hair.

It was almost midnight by the time Saji returned. I was just on my way to bed, my head too heavy to hold upright anymore, when I heard his key in the lock.

"Don't turn the light on," I whispered. "How did you get on. Did you speak to Hama?"

"Yes. But it's not good news, I'm afraid."

"What do you mean? She's still got Omori's memories, hasn't she?" I could see the shine of his eyes in the darkness, the outline of his shoulder against the window behind, but his face was nothing more than shadow. He stood still and silent for a moment. "Hasn't she?" I asked again.

"I told her that Tokai wanted to train Omori early, that we wanted her to keep hold of the memories for a little bit longer. But things have been bad for her. Her husband passed away, and she's not doing well. She ran up some big debts, and with the stress of her husband passing, she found that holding the memories was just too much for her. She needed the money, and she needed a clear head. She sold them, Senetsu."

"What? You said that we could trust her."

"How could I have possibly known this would happen?"

I saw his silhouette shift. I didn't need to accuse him, to blame him, I knew him well enough. He'd never forgive himself for this.

"Who did she sell them to?"

"A merchant. She gave me his number."

"And?"

"I called, but he'd already sold the memories on. And he didn't know who to."

"Are you kidding me?"

Saji didn't respond.

"Omori's memories are just gone? She can never be a trader without them, Saji. Her life is over. And... and she'll never, ever know her sister."

He stepped forward and took hold of my arms. "No. I won't let that happen. We need to tell Omori the truth. About everything. And we need to tell her every single day about what an amazing sister she has. I won't let her not know Kioto. We need to tell her. And then we'll all go and get Kioto. Together."

I fell into his arms and sobbed in the darkness.

42

KIOTO

I watched Malia as she writhed on the bed. She'd been screaming for almost an hour. Names and words, but none of it made sense.

I didn't try to quiet her; it was pointless anyway. Her shivers were so bad that she barely even saw or heard me anymore. She was locked into a world where all she knew was the memories she carried. She hadn't eaten, and she'd barely drunk for almost three days.

I looked up at Narata. "Is there anything we can do?"

She shook her head slowly. "Not now. She's too far gone. Why didn't you tell me earlier?"

"I thought I'd made her better. She seemed so

much better. I took some memories off her when we were in the police station, and it really worked to ease her shivers. But now… look at her."

"It doesn't work like that, Kioto. Omori's the only one who can help Malia now. The only way to stop the shivers is to remove all her memories in one go. All of them. You can't do it a bit at a time. It doesn't work. It just makes things worse. All you did was to put your own life in danger."

"Is she worse now because I took some memories?"

Narata nodded. "We can't know for certain, but it's a strong possibility." She rubbed my shoulder. "I'm sorry."

"Then we need to get Omori. Now."

"We have to tread carefully. We need her to agree to do this. If she refuses, there's really no way that we can make her do it. I just don't know how we're going to convince her."

"Surely she'll listen to me."

"She doesn't even know who you are."

"What?"

"The memories that were taken from her were all of her memories of you. She doesn't even know that you exist."

"Why would my parents want her to forget about me?"

"Maybe it was too painful for her to be apart from you. You must remember; the pair of you were inseparable."

"So, I need to convince Omori that I, a perfect

stranger, am her sister, and that she needs to come and perform an extraction that would kill any other trader, so that she can train up as a vessel to help rogues to kill others like her? And eventually, they'll kill her too. I can tread as carefully as anything, but she'd have to be out of her mind to agree to that."

"If you can't convince her, then Malia will die, and Omori will never be a trader. And she won't know you either."

43

KIOTO

"I'm not really meant to be seen out and about in the city," I explained to Dai. "It was kind of a condition of us being released by the police. Y'know, to make ourselves scarce pretty quickly. I'm certainly not meant to be hanging around in these kind of places."

Dai sat on the bench and pulled me down to sit beside him.

"It wasn't a condition of your release," he said.

"Yeah, it kind of was."

"Why do you think they released you all of a sudden?"

I shrugged. "Because they had nothing solid to hold us on?"

Dai raised an eyebrow. "Do you really think they

need something solid to hold a trader? There are traders who have been in prison for years without being charged for anything at all. The system doesn't give a shit about people like you. You got released, because I had a word in the right ear."

I snorted. "What? And the system gives two hoots about a filthy rogue?"

"Not all rogues are filthy. And I happen to be a rogue with a lot of friends in high places."

"How do you have 'friends in high places'?"

"I do a lot of favours for people. And I always expect them to pay me back. You'd be surprised at the connections I have."

We were sat in a small square, the corners of which were marked with boxed-in gardens; a few flowers, a few shrubs, neatly clipped back. A hint of nature, without it becoming intrusive. Several coffee shops and restaurants surrounded the space, their tables and chairs sprawling across the pavement, competing for space. They were the kind of establishments that sold homemade, organic cakes alongside their organic coffee in recycled cups. Nothing processed, nothing mass-produced. All so that people could feel better about themselves, pretend that they were somehow superior, that they weren't just consumer robots seduced by slick advertising. That sipping this coffee made them different, even though, while they drank, they also shopped on the net, buying all the crap they didn't need but were told they did.

"My sister comes here?" I asked.

"Almost every day," Dai replied. He nodded to a coffee shop in front of us. "Skinny latte with vanilla syrup."

"Really?"

Dai laughed and punched me playfully on the arm. "I don't know! But, yeah, she comes here quite regularly."

I frowned and rubbed my arm, shuffling further away from him. We weren't friends or comrades, he'd made it clear that I was under his control, even if he did refuse to use the word 'prisoner'.

He looked at me. "I guess our relationship isn't very standard, is it?"

I frowned at my boots and said nothing.

"Look, in a way, every single relationship is screwed up. There's always some kind of power dynamic." He shrugged. "Why should ours be any different? But you don't need to be so serious about it."

"About your threats to kill me and everyone close to me if I try to leave? Sure, why would I ever be 'serious' about that?"

"You really need to lighten up."

I huffed. "What is it with you people? Why do you always say that? You kill traders for sport. Why should I take that lightly? And how can you take it so lightly?"

"We don't do it for sport."

"Then, why do you do it?"

Dai looked at me for a moment, his mouth a hard, straight line. And then he looked past me,

233

focussing on something past my shoulder.

I turned around.

"There she is," Dai said.

I didn't know what I'd expected—some kind of bolt of recognition, some kind of psychic explosion, something monumental, something to mark this moment as earth-shattering, world-shaking—but nothing happened. I simply watched a teenage girl, who looked a bit like my sister did, walk across the square. I'd imagined this moment, running through hundreds of possibilities; emotional breakdowns, outbursts of rage, running, hugging, crying. But I had never once imagined an emotional void, a moment no more significant than passing a stranger in the street.

"What now?" I whispered, more to myself than to Dai.

Omori looked up, her eyes at first skimming past us, but they snapped back, and focussed. She stopped, stared for a moment, and then hurried back the way she came.

I stood up. Dai stood up next to me, laying one hand gently on my arm.

"She saw us," I said. "Did you see that?" I looked at Dai, but he simply shrugged in reply. "Did you see the way she looked at us?" I urged.

"What?"

"She knew me. She knew who I was. Why would she stop and stare like that otherwise? She knew me." It took some effort to stop myself bouncing up and down like an excited toddler. They'd taken all of her memories away, but, somehow, somewhere deep inside of herself, Omori knew me.

"Don't be ridiculous," said Dai. "A trader and a rogue out together? That's something to stare at. Everyone was staring."

44

SENETSU

Saji charged through the front door, stumbling over the mat, and practically falling into the kitchen. He grabbed the back of one of the dining chairs and managed to come to a stop. His eyes were wide, his face pale, his breathing ragged.

"What's happened?" I asked.

"Liberation," he gasped, pointing towards the open front door. "Liberation."

"Omori!" I screamed.

But the officers were already at the door, they were already pouring in like a dam had broken.

I raced forward, my hands up, trying, somehow, to stem the flow. But it pushed me to one side like a twig.

Omori appeared and stood, mouth gaping.

"Run!" I screamed, but she couldn't move. Her feet were rooted to the spot, her mouth flapping open and closed.

I reached out, and my hands scrabbled against uniforms and button and boots. I was on all fours, staring through legs as they took hold of my daughter and marched her back across the room.

"Mummy!" she cried out, fighting against the hands that held her. But what chance did a five year old have?

Saji took hold of her shoulders, tried to wrench her free. I crawled forward, touched the edge of one of her shoes.

"Don't you take her!" I screamed, the words choked with tears.

Without any warning, a stun gun whistled, and I saw Saji's body lurch. I heard him drop to the floor, but I couldn't see him, couldn't get to him. The stun gun whistled again, and he cried out.

"Stop," I begged. "Stop!"

The uniforms and the boots retreated, and Omori's shoe slipped away from my fingers. I scrambled to my feet and followed them, pulling at any arm I could find.

"Don't take her, don't take her!"

Through the crowd of officers, I saw Tokai, arms crossed, watching.

"Tokai!" I cried. "They're taking Omori!"

Tokai didn't respond. I grabbed hold of her.

"They're taking Omori, help us!"

She didn't move.

I threw myself at the uniforms then, clawing, biting, scratching, tearing at anything my fingers could grab hold of. A stun gun whistled, and the ground found me. I stared up at the sky above, my body unresponsive to my desperate pleas for it to move. All I could feel was pain, burning through me. I heard the slamming of doors, the hum of auto-cars, and the screams of my daughter.

45

KIOTO

I stroked Malia's forehead as she whimpered in her sleep. Her face and arms were striped with scratches, her cheeks were pale and sunken, her breathing rapid.

I looked up at Narata.

"What are we going to do?" I asked.

Narata shook her head slowly. "We need Omori."

"I don't even know how to start with convincing her to come here."

"You don't have to," Dai said. He was leaning against the door frame, arms folded. "We'll just grab her. Problem solved."

"That is not the problem solved at all," said Narata. "We need her to be compliant, to agree to being trained up. If you drag her here against her will, Malia will die anyway."

"Let me speak to her," I said. "I have to try."

"Then what are you waiting around for?" Dai asked. "Go speak to your sister. Convince her if you think you can. But if you don't, then we'll do things my way. And don't worry about her refusing to train, I can get her to agree to it." He flashed me a smile. "One way or another."

46

SENETSU

"How could you just stand there and say nothing?" I was clinging to Tokai's dress like a child pleading for ice cream. I was aware that everyone in the community hut was staring, but I didn't care. All I could think about was Omori.

Tokai pushed my hands away, but I simply clung on elsewhere instead.

"She's my daughter, and I'll never see her again."

"You are causing a scene, Senetsu."

"I don't care. You have to do something, you have to help us."

Tokai finally looked down at me. She took hold of my hands and pulled me up to my feet. Somehow, they managed to hold my weight.

"Please, Tokai, please," I wailed.

"Get a grip on yourself. Have some self respect."

"I've lost both my daughters," I snapped.

"Yes, you do seem to have a problem holding onto them."

I took a step back from her. "How can you say that?"

Tokai didn't reply, but looked at me with eyes completely devoid of empathy.

"Why didn't you step in?" I demanded.

"Because this may be the best thing for Omori."

"What? How?"

"You were standing in the way of her progress."

"Well, she'll never make any progress now, will she? She'll be adopted into a citizen family, and every trace of her trader routes will be educated out of her. She'll never be able to find her way back to us, and we'll never be able to find her. You've lost the vessel you wanted so badly."

"Actually, I know exactly where she is."

"You're lying."

"Why would I lie about that? I arranged her adoption."

"Tell me where she is."

"I will not."

I stepped back towards her, my fists clenched tightly. "Yes, you will."

"What are you going to do, Senetsu? Attack your own brood mother in front of everyone?"

I looked around us. The men had stood up from their tables, and several had moved closer, their bodies poised for action.

"Then they need to know exactly who you are," I said loudly. "They need to know that you arranged that liberation. That you're trafficking trader children."

Tokai held her hands out and gestured to the rest of the room. "Oh dear, Senetsu, I don't think anyone believes you."

She was right. Or, at least, no one was surprised.

"They were all in on it too, weren't they?"

"Everyone here is willing to do whatever is best for the colony. Even if it's a difficult decision."

"What's best for the colony?" I looked around at the other faces. "You stole my daughter. How could any of you do that?" I looked to the women, the mothers with their children sat next to them. "How could you take a child away from her parents? How could that be best for anyone?"

"Omori is safe. And she will be returned to us when the time is right."

I stared at Tokai. It was like being in a nightmare where no one could hear you speak. Where you could scream as loud as you could, but no sound came out of you.

"You've all lost your minds. All of you." I jabbed the air with my finger. "I am going to get Kioto. You can't stop me now. And when I come back, you will tell me where Omori is."

"This is the best way to protect your daughter, you'll see that eventually."

"No. I am the best person to protect her." I

prodded my chest. "Me. She should be with me."

"You've already mutilated her."

"What?"

"You've mutilated her mind. Don't think I don't know about the little extraction in Akimori. As soon as I get those memories back, Omori will be trained as a vessel. In the meantime, I will be keeping you as far away from her as I can. You've done enough damage to her already."

"You've done nothing to keep her safe."

Tokai shook her head slowly. "You've been trusting all the wrong people. Maybe it's time you learnt the truth. Maybe that will help you see that this is the right decision." She turned and walked towards the door. "Come with me. I want to show you something."

As we stepped outside, she took hold of my hand. It wasn't a gesture of solidarity or support, it was simply to hold me still.

"I had a visitor today," she said. "Look."

I looked the way she had nodded and saw Narata.

"She's alive?" I whispered.

"Yes, your precious Okaporo brood mother. She got out before the rogues massacred everyone in Okaporo. How lucky that she managed to save herself. How unfortunate that she couldn't save anyone else."

"She saved me, and Saji, and Omori."

"Watch."

As Narata left the confines of the colony, three

men greeted her. They stood and talked for a moment, heads together, co-conspirators. And then I heard it. The terrifyingly familiar roar of a petrol motor starting up. There was only one group of people that still used the old hybrid engines. Rogues.

I looked at Tokai.

Tokai nodded. "She saved a lot of the children too, and the rooks. Because she knew the massacre was coming. She knew, because she ordered it."

47

KIOTO

I'd barely got through the door of the coffee shop when a waitress hurried over to me and ushered me back outside.

"We can't serve you," she said, and her apologetic tone even sounded genuine. "The owner, he's... he doesn't like traders. I just don't think you're in the right part of the city."

"Don't I know it," I muttered.

I buried my hands into my pockets and skulked over to one of the benches. I sat down and leaned back. A watery sun was trying its best to break through the clouds, but I didn't hold out too much hope for its endeavours. This place didn't deserve sunshine anyway.

I tugged my hood up over my hair and sat, slumped forward, one hand cradling my chin while my elbow teetered on my knee.

When I'd come looking for Omori, it had been like an exciting quest to reunite long-lost family. I'd been certain that it would end in happy tears and hugs that you never wanted to end. But right now, part of me didn't even want her to show up. Part of me never wanted to see her again. The rogues simply wanted to use her, use her as a death warrant for other vessels. I just didn't know how much I could really trust Narata. My entire heart was split in two, and I couldn't see a way to reconcile those halves. I wanted to trust her. I wanted to believe that she could get us all away from the rogues safely, but there was a doubt that refused to dissipate. I had to listen to it. It was those doubts that refused to be silenced, that sense of scepticism, of wariness, that had kept me alive.

Traders didn't wander far from their colonies. They had a certain level of protection there, and that protection fell away as soon as they left the confines of home.

I didn't look up as someone sat on the bench next to me. I could smell their organic coffee, and it was just as bitter as any other.

"Hello, Kioto," they said after a moment.

My head snapped up. "Omori," I said.

"It is you."

I nodded. "It is."

She took a deep breath and exhaled it slowly

before speaking again.

"I'd like you to leave Kumonayo. Leave me alone to live my life."

"Is that what you really want?"

She shifted, turning towards me. "Yes."

"I thought you'd want to see me."

"Not really. I'm sorry. I'm sure you imagined this differently."

I nodded. "A little bit, yeah." We sat in silence for a moment. The conversation had nowhere else to go, but neither of us moved to leave.

"I didn't think you knew who I was," I said at last.

"I know who you are. I know who, and what I am. Our parents told me everything. How they had my memories taken, and then they were lost. They were keen for me to know who you were though. They showed me loads of photos too. Only up until you were eight, of course, that's why I wasn't absolutely certain that it was you."

"Your friend in the colony told me where to find you. She said you told her once that, if I ever showed up, she should help me find you. So you must have wanted to meet me at some point."

Omori shrugged. "I guess I did then."

"What did you want to say to me?"

She sighed, lolling her head backwards. "I don't know, Kioto. It was years ago. I was just a child."

"But now you don't want to see me?"

"I want to move forward with my life. I don't want to go back to all that." Her hand raised to her right eye, three fingers extended.

"But it's who you are."

"No. It's who you are. A sister I have no true memories of. And it's who our parents are. Parents I don't remember too well either. It's not who I am."

"It is. Whether you like it or not."

"Then it's not who I choose to be. I have a stable life here. Parents who look after me. I have friends, an education, a future. There's nothing for me in the colonies except a whole load of lies."

"Lies?"

"Everyone's lied to me. Or, at least, someone has every time. I wouldn't know what's the truth and what isn't."

"Did you know that our parents are dead?"

Omori dropped her focus to the floor and shook her head. "I don't even know how I'm supposed to feel about that," she whispered.

"There's nothing you're supposed to feel. Whatever you're feeling is the correct response. That's what's real. That's what you can trust."

She looked back at me. "Then I feel nothing. Look, our parents told me all these amazing stories about you. They talked about how brave, and clever, and beautiful you are. They said that we were inseparable, like one child with two bodies. They made you sound like the big sister anyone would dream of having. But no one can be that perfect."

"No one is. We used to fight a lot too. I used to tease you until you pulled my hair, then I'd go crying to Mum and get you into trouble." I shrugged. "We were sisters. We did what sisters do."

"But then Tokai started telling me different things about you. About Okaporo. She said that our parents favoured you, that they had always loved you more than me. She said that they'd wished that you had been the vessel so that they could have left me behind instead."

"That's not true—"

Omori held up her hand. "It made sense to me, because all our parents talked about was you, and how amazing you were, and how much they loved you." She dropped her hands into her lap and stared at them. "It made so much sense."

"What else did Tokai tell you?"

"She told me that you were jealous of me being the vessel. That you hated me for being the special one. She said that you told the rogues where I was because you wanted them to kill me. That you caused the massacre."

My fists gripped the front edge of the bench. "I don't believe it. That's not true at all." I felt angry tears rise up from my stomach, pressing at the backs of my eyes. I didn't want to cry. I didn't want Omori to mistake it for guilt. "I lost everything in the massacre. Everything."

"I'd mostly dismissed that too. It seemed too far fetched for an eight year old. But then, I saw you sat here with that rogue the other day, and I thought that it must be true after all."

"No, he's—" I clamped my mouth shut. I couldn't tell her that he was my captor, not when I needed her to agree to come with me. I dropped my head into my hands. "Urgh, I can't explain. You just need to trust me."

"That's the whole problem. Everyone wants me to trust them, but they only tell me half truths, or no truths at all."

"I love you, Omori, and for eleven years I thought that you were dead. I thought my whole family was dead. I thought that Okaporo was lost altogether. But, suddenly, you're back in my life, and I love you just as much as I ever did. I want no harm to come to you. I would gladly give my life for yours. I promised you that on the day you were born, and I don't intend to break that promise."

The words weren't good enough. The emotion was boiling inside me, pressing into every vein, pushing its way through me. And I needed to get it out, but I couldn't find adequate sentiments for its escape.

Omori shook her head slowly. "It's just words, Kioto. And they're easy enough."

I exhaled. "Actually, you'd be surprised."

"What were you expecting to find after so long? Me desperate to return to the life I once had?"

"I don't know. Maybe. Look, I have your memories. I can restore them for you. If you can't trust anyone else, surely you can trust yourself. Once you have them, you can make up your mind about everything."

She frowned. "How do you have them?"

I held my hands up defensively. "Purely by coincidence. Or luck, or even fate perhaps. I stumbled across a merchant, and his smudger had them."

"A slave?"

"Yes. I bought her. So we can restore all of them to you. You won't have to piece your life together through things that other people tell you. Or don't tell you."

"I don't know. I feel weird about the whole process. Having someone digging around inside my brain, looking at whatever they want."

"It's not like that. I wouldn't do that."

She smiled bitterly. "But I'd have to trust you."

I nodded. "I've got one of your memories, the smudger, Malia, still has the rest. Just let me give you this one memory, and you can see what the process is like. It will take mere seconds, if you're open to it. Memories want to return home. It will slip into your brain, and you'll barely even notice it happening."

Omori exhaled deeply. Her eyes flicked from side to side as she thought it over. She nodded quickly, just the once.

"Close your eyes," I said. "And you need to relax. Don't fight me. Just accept the memory, and we're done."

Omori closed her eyes and nodded again.

"Are you ready?" I asked.

She nodded.

I placed my hand on her forehead and closed my own eyes. She resisted me, pushed me back out. Her mind was locked shut. This wasn't a technique any normal citizen knew. This was something she'd been taught, and she'd been taught well.

"Relax," I whispered. "You're blocking me."

The block tentatively gave way, softening, until I was able to push my way through it. Omori's memory rushed out of my head without any instruction or coaxing at all. It knew where it really belonged. As soon as it was gone, I withdrew. As I did, I felt her barrier return.

Omori blinked several times before her eyes focussed back on me.

"How did that feel?" I asked her.

"Weird. But not that unpleasant."

"Who taught you to block your mind like that? That's not something you just do automatically."

Omori looked at the floor. "I'm not supposed to tell anyone about it."

I put my hand on her leg. "It can be our secret. We used to have lots of secrets together. We had a little notebook that we used to write them in. We decided to bury it once, and the next day it poured with rain. When we dug it up again, it was nothing more than mush."

"It's weird having this memory back. It feels like mine, but not like mine all at once."

"It'll settle after a day or two. But it can feel a little weird at first."

She shrugged. "I guess it's a happy memory."

"We always used to sleep in the same bed. We would whisper stories in the darkness until we fell asleep."

She nodded.

"Would you like the rest of your memories

back?" I asked.

"I don't know." She sighed. "That probably sounds so wrong, but I've lived most of my life without them, and this one feels like it belongs, but doesn't. I don't know, it's not exactly a nice feeling. It feels like another lie somehow. Something else I'm expected to trust."

"But if you have the rest as well—"

"Please don't push me, Kioto. This is my head, and it's my decision."

"I'm sorry. You're right. It's just—" I fell silent.

"What?"

"No, forget it, it's not your problem, and I don't want you to feel pressured into anything."

"Tell me."

"Malia, the smudger, she's got the shivers. Really badly. She's going to die."

"Unless I take my memories back."

"It's not enough. She needs to be emptied of everything she's carrying. She needs a vessel."

"But I'm not—" Realisation darkened across her face. "You want me to train up so that I can save her."

"Actually, strictly speaking, you can't be trained with memories missing. But you can be talked through the process. As soon as your memories are back in your head, while the others flow away, then you can be trained."

Omori turned and stared across the square. We sat quietly for some time, watching people go into the coffee shops, buying hot drinks, pastries, bagels, carrying them out in recycled paper bags.

Omori stood. "I need to think about this." And then she was gone.

48

KIOTO

Omori had barely vacated her seat when Dai dropped into it, stepping over the back of the bench.

"How did it go?" he asked.

"I really don't know." I could still feel the warmth of Omori's forehead on my hand.

"So... she didn't agree to anything?"

"She agreed to think about it. With what I've thrown at her today, that's probably better than we could have hoped for."

"Well, she better not spend too long thinking about it."

"We're asking a lot of her."

He shrugged. "If you say so."

I opened my mouth, but then closed it again.

There was no point in arguing. Despite the trader blood that flowed through him, Dai had absolutely no empathy for us. Perhaps that was the only way he could justify what he did. He couldn't let empathy get in his way.

"Do you think you can close the deal, or what?"

"'Close the deal'? This decision will change the rest of her life. It's a big choice to make."

Dai smiled. "But, of course, you and I both know that she doesn't really have the choice. Don't we? Besides, your smudger is dying. So, if you want your sister back, you need to hurry along this little decision of hers. Neither of us can afford to have her mull it over for too long."

"I guess not."

"And we need her trained up quickly. I've got a lead on another vessel, so we need to move soon. They don't tend to hang around in one place for too long, especially if they get wind that we're after them."

"Just give her some time."

"Like I said, we don't have that luxury." He cracked his knuckles. "I could just grab her if I wanted to. Job done."

"You know why you can't do that," I snapped. "I'll convince her, just leave it to me."

"You seem very sure of yourself all of a sudden."

"I don't want to see her get hurt. Who knows what will happen if you go in there guns blazing. I want my sister back, even if it's not the way I imagined it will be."

Dai leaned back. "Think you can run, do you?"

"What?"

"I know what you're planning. You and Narata."

"We're not planning anything." My heart was hammering. I was certain he'd hear it.

"Train Omori up, and then make a break for it. You probably have some half-baked romantic notion of setting up the Okaporo colony again."

"That's not true."

"Look, I've known Narata almost her entire life. I know her almost as well as I know myself. And I know when she's planning something."

"If she is, I know nothing about it."

He patted me on the leg and laughed. "Don't bother denying it." He shrugged. "Do it. I dare you. Just try to run." He turned to face me. "You will always be watched, you will always be heard. Even when you think you're alone."

49

SENETSU

I stepped back and gripped hold of the railing beside me. My head was swimming, not quite believing what my eyes were reporting, but unable to deny it too.

"I'm sorry that you had to see that," said Tokai, without an ounce of sorrow in her tone. "But you needed to know the truth. Narata's been in league with rogues almost her entire life."

I shook my head. My mouth made the motion to say "no", but there was no sound available for it.

"I know it's hard to accept," Tokai continued, "but it's true. You've just seen it yourself. As you know, Narata grew up in a liberation orphanage, but what you don't know is that she grew up alongside a rogue. A boy called Dai. He was born on a colony, but became the worst kind of traitor. And he poisoned Narata's mind too. He's the leader of a rogue gang now, a particularly nasty one responsible for hundreds of trader deaths. I wouldn't be surprised if he didn't shed some blood with his own hands in Okaporo."

I shook my head again. My hand slipped from the railing and I found myself on my knees without the strength to get back up.

"Narata came here today to find Omori, to kill her. You see how vital it was that I had her liberated? If Narata had knocked on your door, you'd have let the wolf right into your home without even knowing it. But I kept your daughter safe. I protected her. Narata tried to rip the information from me, using her training as a weapon against a fellow trader. The worst kind of traitor. But in the struggle, I managed to rip her memories of Omori being here from her head. I protected her. And now Narata will never be able to find her."

I nodded, my eyes brimming with tears. Everything I'd ever trusted in had turned out to be a lie. The one person I thought I could trust above all others, turned out to be an enemy.

Tokai crouched down and rubbed my back. "I told you that you could trust me, Senetsu. I told you that I was doing the right thing for Omori."

"I can't... I can't..." I sobbed. I didn't even know the words to explain the devastation that was sweeping through me. My entire past had become a wasteland, a battleground long after the dead had been buried. It was a dried up lake, a felled forest, a derelict town. Everything had been scooped out of me. The very essence of everything I was, my understanding of myself, my foundations, and everything I'd ever built on them. Everything was gone in just the briefest of moments. An entire lifetime erased in just a couple of minutes. I was a hole. A vast, gaping, empty maw.

"It's hard to accept, I know. Maybe you need to see it for yourself. I have Narata's ripped memories in a young trader in my house. There's some information in them that I think you'll find enlightening."

I shook my head and raised a defensive hand. I didn't have the stomach for any more truth right now.

Tokai took hold of my hand. "I think you'll find it helpful. A place that you can restart. Rebuild." She pulled me to my feet. "Come on, you really need to see this."

My feet followed Tokai's, but my mind wasn't in control. It was racing through everything. Cataloguing, analysing, ordering every memory I had. I was looking for a clue, a sign that I might have missed. Something that may have seemed innocuous at the time, but would now hold weight and importance. I was looking for a whiff of betrayal. Searching for a needle of treachery. And all the while, I was hoping I would find none. Hoping that this was just a terrible misunderstanding. A muddle that, one day, we'd be able to laugh about.

Tokai lifted my hand and placed it on the trader's forehead. I was so numb that I could barely feel her skin under my fingers. I pushed forward into her mind, looking for the memory that she should be pushing forward to me. But she wasn't. Nothing was illuminated. I looked around in the darkness of her mind. And then I saw a light, and I made my way towards it. As I did, the space around me became floodlit. Every memory was ablaze and flowing towards me.

I opened my eyes and looked at the girl in front of me. Her pale blue eyes, her flawless skin. No scars. She wasn't a trader. She was a carrier. A smudger.

Tokai's arm shook as she held my hand against the smudger's head.

"That's right, Senetsu," she whispered. "Don't try to fight it, just let those memories in."

It was far too late for fighting. The rush had begun.

50

KIOTO

A light drizzle chilled me as I sat on the bench watching the coffee shops again. It ached its way through to my bones. My toes felt like wood, and my hands, despite being pushed deep into my pockets were raw with the cold.

My phone buzzed again, and I reluctantly pulled it out, exposing my hands to the icy damp once more.

'Malia's really bad. She's not even aware that I'm here anymore. Any sign of Omori at all?'

I pushed my phone back into my pocket without replying. After all, what was I going to say? The situation hadn't changed. We were waiting for a miracle when we had no time to wait.

I looked back across the square, watching people

closely. Looking to see if I could spot someone watching me. I could feel eyes on me all the time. If Dai had been bluffing about the surveillance, it had worked perfectly. I'd been eaten up by paranoia ever since.

I analysed the movements of every passer by. Tried to see under their hoods, hats, and umbrellas. Who were they? What were they doing here? Did they just glance at me?

Another message.

'There's nothing I can do for her anymore. She doesn't respond to anything. The shivers have taken over completely.'

I frowned. What could I do?

"Come on, Omori," I muttered, pulling my hood further forward. The front edge of it was sodden, and the drizzle gathered there as droplets.

This was hopeless. All I was doing was freezing to the bone for nothing.

My phone buzzed.

'I think she may only have a few hours left. You should be here at the end for her.'

I grunted, and punched in a quick reply.

'Of course. I'm on my way.'

51

KIOTO

I'd never felt so helpless. All I could do was hold Malia's hand as the shivers ate away the final pieces of her. I could only hope that somewhere, somehow, she knew that I was there for her.

Narata was laying out an altar, ready to assist Malia's passing into the afterworld. We wanted her to have a trader's passing. That, at least, we could do for her.

A bowl of herbs smouldered, filling the room with wisps and curls of sweet-smelling smoke.

I wiped at my face, but it was pointless: the tears were streaming out of me, and there was no stopping them.

I lay my head against Malia's and whispered to

her. "I ask that you find peace in the afterworld, that the shivers leave you along with any memories, either yours or others, of this physical world. Let your soul fly, Malia."

I wrapped my arms around her and squeezed her tightly. The convulsions and shouting had ceased, and she lay still, her breathing short and shallow. She was looking into the afterworld now, seeing with her soul instead of her eyes. At least she would be free.

I looked up at Narata who nodded gently at me. I sat up and lifted Malia's head into my lap.

The bedroom door opened and Dai stepped in. He looked at me and grinned.

"Do you mind?" I snapped. "You, of all people, are not welcome here right now."

"I have some news you might like to hear."

I made a show of sighing deeply. "What could possibly be more important than this?"

"You have a visitor."

I glanced at Narata. "What? Who?"

"Your sister is here."

I stood in the corridor outside and waited impatiently as Omori was brought up to us.

"You came," I said as she rounded the corner.

"I did."

"Does this mean you want to train up?"

Omori shook her head. "My whole past is nothing but lies, and I want nothing to do with it. I'm sorry."

I swallowed back more tears. "Does that include me?"

Omori nodded quickly. "I'm sorry, Kioto. I've actually made a new life for myself, and I want to be allowed to live it. I need to move forward."

"Then why are you here?"

"I want to help your smudger. She doesn't deserve to die for something that someone else did to her. Plus, I can complete my own story."

I led Omori into the bedroom and closed the door behind us.

"Let's do this," I said to Narata.

Omori looked over at Malia on the bed. "Is she…?"

"Not quite, but she doesn't have long," Narata said. "You arrived just in time."

"I followed Kioto back here. I stood outside for so long trying to decide whether to come in or not."

I reached out and squeezed Omori's hand. "I'm so glad you did."

She pulled her hand away. "I only did it to save her. No one deserves to die like this."

Narata stepped forward and placed her hand on Omori's shoulder. "I'll talk you through the whole process. It should be simple enough. Your own memories want to return. They'll come out with practically no work on your part at all. The others will follow. It will be fast and forceful."

"A rush," Omori whispered.

I looked up at her. How did she know that word?

"That's right," Narata continued. "You have to try not to panic, and don't break the connection. Just let them flow through you."

"Let's get started," I said.

Narata knelt in front of her altar.

"We don't have time for that," I said.

"There's always time to do things properly." She tapped the floor beside her and I dutifully knelt.

As we completed the Dedication, I watched Omori from under half-closed lids. She sat on the edge of the bed, hands in her lap, eyes closed. She mouthed the words along with us.

When the Dedication was finished, Narata rose and took Omori's hand gently in hers. She placed her other hand on top.

"Are you ready?" she asked.

"I guess so," Omori replied.

She followed Narata to the side of the bed.

"One hand here," Narata pressed Omori's hand onto Malia's stomach. "And the other here." She placed Omori's other hand on Malia's forehead. "That's the important one. That's how the memories are transferred. The other one—" she pointed to Malia's stomach "—that's more of a comforting thing, to stop your extractee from panicking, or from feeling too detached from the physical world. Merchants don't use the second hand. That's just something traders do. Now, when we start the transfer, it will come slowly at first, but when the rush comes it might feel a bit like you're drowning. But it's only for a few seconds. Don't break the connection, and don't panic. Just let it wash over you, keep breathing, and remember that it will pass in just a moment."

Omori nodded.

"Are you ready to begin?"

Omori nodded again.

"I'll start the transfer myself and pass the memories through into you. This is called tandem, or relay extraction. It's not commonly done, we don't even teach this technique anymore, but it's the only way that we can do this today."

I'd never even heard of such a strategy. I couldn't imagine what situations you might want to use it in. Other than this one, of course. But this was hardly regular. I wondered when they stopped teaching it.

"Close your eyes," Narata said. She placed her hand on top of Omori's. "Here we go. Just focus on your breathing. In and out, in and out."

I watched Omori's body tense, and then relax a little. I couldn't remember my first experience of an extraction, I'd done countless of them since. But it was something that you never got used to. Either the feeling of having an intruder inside your own head, or the feeling of being an intruder in someone else's.

She leaned forward slightly when the rush started, as if wading against the current. I thought that I'd feel happy seeing this, validated. This is what I wanted; my sister trading alongside me. Continuing the Okaporo traditions, wherever we were in the world. But that wasn't what I felt. It was more like regret, sorrow, guilt. Had I dragged my sister into a life that I myself hated and despised?

"We're done," Narata said. "How do you feel?"

Omori raised her hand to her head. "Dizzy."

"You're lucky, you won't get the throw like the

rest of us do, because you're not keeping something in your body that doesn't belong. That's what the throw is; your body trying to eject the foreign object. But it's already gone from you."

"Except my own memories."

"Yes. Can you feel them settling back into place?"

"My head feels heavier. Like it's full."

"It's a bit weird, isn't it? Don't worry, that feeling won't last for long."

I stood and crossed to the bed, rubbing Omori's shoulder as I passed her. I took hold of Malia's hand. It was limp, cold. Her fingers tightened slightly around mine.

"What happens to Malia now?" I asked.

"She'll sleep for a long time," Narata said. "Her body has a lot of healing to do. It might be days before she wakes up properly."

"I'll be here when she does." I looked up at Omori. "Thank you. I know it can't have been an easy decision to come."

"I caught a glimpse of some of those memories as they came through my head," Omori said. "I can't believe that she was forced to carry them. It must have been horrible. I want to help. I want to help more people like her."

"Really?" I said. "You want to train up as a vessel?"

"If I get to help people like Malia, then yes. I do."

I looked at Narata. "What do we do now?"

"We bide our time," Narata said. "We wait for our chance."

"Our chance for what?" Omori asked.

I grabbed her hands. "We're going to get away, back to Okaporo. We're going home."

"I don't really remember Okaporo."

"But it's home. Even if you don't feel like it is now. It's our roots. Our ancestors—"

Narata placed her hand over mine and Omori's. "Let's just take one day at a time. All this is very new to everyone. Just slow down, Kioto."

"I just..." I trailed off, looking back and forth between the two of them. I felt like I was about to burst. It seemed like everything I wanted was so close, but was still being held just out of reach.

The door opened and Dai stepped into the room.

"We're ready when you are," he said to Narata. He looked at Malia asleep on the bed. "What are we doing with her?"

"She's coming with us," I said.

Dai frowned and looked at Narata. She nodded once.

"Whatever," he said. "Downstairs in ten, ok? We've got vessels to find."

Omori looked at me and smiled tightly. I squeezed her hand.

I had my sister, right here, and I was no longer alone. I had more of my home, more of anything, than I'd had in years.

Once upon a time, rogues had taken everything from me, and now I'd managed to get a part of it back. I wasn't about to let them take it away again. I closed my eyes and the sound of the ocean filled my ears.

ANGELINE TREVENA

ACKNOWLEDGEMENTS

The original concept for The Smudger was crafted during many a long car journey, and, more pleasantly, during some coffee and very naughty cake in an incredibly quaint little cafe in Worcester. But it wasn't done by me alone. My wonderful alpha reader and soundboard, my ever patient husband, Paul. I couldn't have done it without you.

And it would be amiss of me not to mention our two beautiful boys who slept through those many long car journeys. You two make me laugh every single day. You've tested my wisdom, my patience, and my ability to build train tracks (which I seem to have quite a talent for). You may never know how hard it is to write a book while a toddler tries to pull themselves onto your lap, or how quickly the Mario Kart theme tune can pull you out of a fictional world, but I wouldn't change a thing. I love you both in your weird wonderfulness.

My parents who continue to have faith in me. You taught me to dream, to believe in everything, and you let me read books at the dinner table. And Dad, while the scifi classics you used to read us as bedtime stories were probably a bit inappropriate, you introduced me to speculative fiction and the fantastical worlds I could travel to.

I need to thank the eagle eyes and honest words of Pat Salvant, Bonnie Bishop, Nigel Perels, Kay Smillie, Anne Mullane, Riddhi Padwal, and Alina Hart. With dusters in hand, you buffed and polished this book to what it is now. Thank you all.

My cover artist, Olivia, who proved endless patience in the face of my indecision.

My peers and fellow writers who have encouraged me, pushed me on, supported and advised me. Writing can easily become such a solitary, lonely job, and having someone who understands dealing with unruly characters, discovering gaping plot holes just before bedtime, or the pain and torture of formatting (don't get me started) is so important. It lets me know I'm not alone. And that I'm not completely crazy. Not completely.

And of course, thank you to my wonderful readers. You're the reason I show up every day. Well, that and the coffee.

ABOUT ANGELINE TREVENA

Angeline Trevena was born and bred in a rural corner of Devon, but now lives among the breweries and canals of central England with her husband, their two sons, and a rather neurotic cat. She is a dystopian urban fantasy and post-apocalyptic author, a podcaster, and events manager.

In 2003 she graduated from Edge Hill University, Lancashire, with a BA Hons Degree in Drama and Writing. During this time she decided that her future lay in writing words rather than performing them.

Some years ago she worked at an antique auction house and religiously checked every wardrobe that came in to see if Narnia was in the back of it. She's still not given up looking for it.

Find out more at www.angelinetrevena.co.uk